Bukom

Bill Marshall

Afram Publications (Ghana) Ltd.

First Published in 1979 by:
Longman Group Limited,
Longman House,
Burnt Hill, Harlow,
Essex CM20 2JE,
England

This Edition Published by:
Afram Publications (Ghana) Limited
P.O. Box M18
Accra, Ghana

Tel: +233 244 314 103, +233 302 412 561
Kumasi: +233 501 266 698, +233 322 047 524/5
E-mail: sales@aframpubghana.com
                publishing@aframpubghana.com
Website: www.aframpubghana.com

Cover illustration by: Hawa Olae

ISBN:978 9964 7 0568 8

To my brother, Harry, and sister, Monica

Chapter 1

Ataa Kojo picked his way confidently along the dark alleyways of James Town. He was heading for home. The smile that played on his lips sprang from an inner satisfaction. The spill-over of a pleasant feeling – the feeling a man, any man would experience after having made the grade and gained recognition for it... The recognition need not be absolute. Even a small token was enough. It would put a smile on any man's lips, that would be just the beginning. The rest would follow, and if need be, he would make it follow. People sometimes have to be pushed a little to recognise the unique.

At his age, he had not done badly at all. Five grown-up children, a military service record without blemish, and twenty-five years service with a European trading firm.

He was not quite sober, but he made sure that the gold tiepin was safe in his pocket. He would show it to the whole neighbourhood and prove to them that he was somebody to be respected. From now on, he would impress upon everybody to call him Mr. Bukoni, yes, Mister Kojo Bukoni, and not Ataa Kojo as they call everybody. Twenty-five years of loyal service with the European company had earned him a tiepin and that was no small achievement.

Self-elation and over-exuberance fanned his ego, over-spilling into a song.

'*Onward Christian soldiers,*
Marching as to war...'

The kerosene lamps were burning at Bukom Square and women were selling their *banku* and *domedo*. The fisherfolk were eating their dinner by the street side and pinching the bottoms of the women who passed by. Everything was as it had always been in that part of the town except that Ataa Kojo was wearing a white suit, complete with tie and shoes, and was singing 'Onward Christian soldiers' and no one seemed to notice him. 'Bloody fools! If they knew who I was, they would come and shake my hand and start calling me Mr. Bukoni.' But not to worry, the news would spread in the neighbourhood soon enough and they would know that the director himself had made the presentation and all the big people in the firm who were at the ceremony had clapped their hands. Some of them had taken him to a bar and bought him beer. He had drunk it but it had not meant anything to him; what he was used to was the real thing, the hot stuff Awo Nye sold in her house. He could not understand why folks wasted money on beer.

'Hey, come here, everybody!' Ataa Kojo shouted when he got home. 'Everybody' meant three of his children--, Allotey, Fofo and the last born, 'Chico,' who was still at school. His two eldest children, Martey and Karley, were in Takoradi and Kumasi respectively and did not see their old man except during the Homowo Festival.

'Now where is everybody?' Akaa Kojo shouted again.

'Is that you, father?'

'Yes. Now where are you?'

'In here, father, Allotey shouted back without coming out. Ataa Kojo spat a frothful of alcoholic saliva on the ground and went into the room.

'Where is Fofo?' he asked.

'She hasn't returned from work,' he was told.

'What the devil is she doing in town at this time? I am sure everybody has closed from work by now.'

'Maybe she is doing overtime.' Allotey volunteered this information, knowing well that it would infuriate his father.

'Now don't you give me that nonsense. If that daughter of mine goes and gets herself pregnant, I will have to sack her from this house. Now, why didn't you come to the ceremony?' he asked. And added, 'Foolish, didn't you know the firm was doing me great honour today?'

'Ah yes, what happened?' Allotey asked.

'Oh, you should have been there. The manager said nice things about me.'

'Really?'

'Wait till I show you something,' Ataa Kojo said and dug his hand into his pocket and fished out the little box containing the gold tiepin.

'What is this?' his son asked.

'Open it'

Allotey opened the box and stared at the contents with disappointment.

'Now that is a real gold tiepin, stupid. Twenty-five years of loyal service to that company. That was what the director said.'

Allotey laughed.

'What is funny?'

'But, father, a gold tiepin after twenty-five long years of loyal service to that company is nothing to be excited about.'

'What?'

'My girlfriend gave me a gold chain on my last birthday and that was after I had known her for only two months,' Allotey said proudly.

'Nonsense.'

'Its true.'

'Where is it?'

'Fofo borrowed it last Saturday.'

Ataa Kojo sat down and took off his tie. Should the company have given him something more worthy than a tiepin?

'Dammit, I know some civil servants who stay in service for more than thirty years and yet nobody thinks about them. You are in the civil service yourself and you are still young in it. But you work for twenty-five years and see if you could achieve what I have achieved.'

' I don't envy you, father,' Allotey said.

'You ought to be proud of me. I have given all my children education.'

'Some form of education, you mean. None of us went to the university and that means a lot.'

But the old man impressed upon Allotey that everybody could not go to the university to be worth his salt. He himself had been brought up as the son of a fisherman and had not seen the inside of a classroom.He had learnt how to read and write from Sunday school and from the army, and yet he had been able to make his mark in life.

Even the director had recognised this. As a headman, he had had many workers under him and he had given instructions and they had taken them. He had had to take decisions on his own and inform his superiors; which was more than one could say for the big shots in the Ministries who were afraid to take decisions on their own.

'So who is this girl you have been sleeping with, anyway?' Ataa Kojo asked his son after some time. 'But, father, who said I have been sleeping with a girl?' 'The girl who gave you the chain, don't you sleep with her?'

'No.'

'Liar!'

But that was not a subject Allotey wanted to discuss with his father.

'You must bring her home one day. I must know about such things.'

But Allotey would not take the bait and talk about the girl. He had no intention of bringing her to the house anyway. Not until he had found himself a nice room, far away from the slums of Bukom, where he would have a wireless set and perhaps a record player.

'All right, you can keep mute about it. When she becomes pregnant, I shall get to know about it, sure enough,' Ataa Kojo said.

Fofo arrived home, her new pair of 'woodies' clapping the floor with such noise that Allotey knew his sister had arrived.

'Fofo!' he called.

Fofo entered the room and noticed her father wearing his white suit.

'Hey, who had a wedding?' she asked.

'What do you mean?' her brother asked.

'Well, father never wears his white suit unless there is something special.'

'Well, there is something special. Today, our father was presented with a gold tiepin by the company for twenty-five years of loyal service,' Allotey told his sister.

'Oh yes, I wanted to come. How did it go?'

But the old man did not want to talk about it anymore. He said his son thought it was nothing to boast about.

'Allotey, you can be nasty about things sometimes. We ought to be proud about a thing like that. Who knows, tomorrow his picture might appear in the newspaper.'

'The press men were there,' the old man volunteered.

'You see.'

Allotey then asked his sister where she had been.

'I went to see a friend.'

'A boy?'

'None of your business,' Fofo said.

'Well, I know it is none of my business, but father would like to know about such things.'

'I am sure father can speak for himself,' she said.

Allotey waited for his father to ask Fofo himself, but the old man did not.

'By the way, Fofo, where is the chain you borrowed last Saturday?'

Fofo told him that she had given it to her boyfriend.

'What?'

'Well, it was his birthday and I had nothing to give him so...'

'So you gave him the chain my girlfriend has given me?' Allotey asked.

'Well, yes.'

'Let me tell you something, little woman, you go and get me my chain or you'll be sorry in this house,' he said angrily and got up.

'Where are you going?' she asked.

'None of your business, I am taking my father out for a drink. Father, lets go for a drink. Today I want to buy you a drink and make you real happy.'

'Well, I'm coming too,' Fofo said, and followed the two men outside.

Chapter 2

When Chico returned home from school, he found the place dark and deserted. He threw his books onto a chair and went to the toilet to urinate.

The stench which assailed his nostrils as he opened the door forced him to spend less time there than he wanted. He had never liked using the toilet in the house anyway. He had always saved that ritual till he got to school and used the more civilised flush system on the compound. There, you were not choked by the stench and the buzz of noisy flies. There, you never left a trace after the ritual. All you did after an intimate session with nature was to pull a chain or press a lever and the water came rushing in a torrent to claim its burden and wash everything away down the hole, leaving only clear water behind.

That, to him, was civilisation. That was enlightment and not the box-and-bucket ensemble which could be found in almost every home in the Bukom neighbourhood.

And then there were the lazy sanitary labourers who would not come and remove the darn thing regularly. They would walk into the house any time they felt like it and bother folks in the house to mind how they used the place.

'You make the work hard for us,' they would complain.

'We try not to.'

'Well, you peoples no try hard enough. I fit buy soap for myself, you know. And you peoples no give me nothing for buy soap for myself.'

'But my father gave you twenty only last week.'

'Ahaa, but you say last week. You think how much twenty fit buy? I for wash myself every day. Or you don't know?'

'Well, my father is not in now. Come tomorrow.'

The man would grunt and leave. But it was a sure thing that he would show his face 'tomorrow' to resume the conversation when father was in.

Chicho came out of the toilet and spat. He then made straight for the kitchen. The space created in his stomach after two hours of playing tennis must be filled. He explored the kitchen and discovered a ball and a half of kenkey, cold and hard. He looked into the other pans for something to go with the kenkey. He drew a blank. 'Damn!' he swore, and checked the money in his pocket. He counted the pennies and realised that he had just enough to buy some fried fish to go with the kenkey. He would have preferred *domedo*, but then that was more expensive. He wondered why. But this was not the time to debate why pork was more expensive than fish. People simply did not know that he preferred pork to fried fish.

He walked out of the house, leaving the door open. The dimly lit street, the smoke and the noise from the square were not unfamiliar.

'Aashieee Keleweee!'

There was a long queue of people waiting to buy the *kelewele* and it did not look as if the red plantain chips frying in the pan would be enough to go round all the customers. But she kept on barking, releasing saliva into the boiling pan.

Chico walked past them. He wished he could buy some as dessert but it was not the time for that. He could have a sweet another time when he had money in his pocket. As he walked past the banku stand, the woman behind it called out to him.

'Young man, come and buy banku,' the woman called again.

'I ain't buying banku.'

'What are you buying?' the woman asked.

'None of your business,' the boy said.

The woman did not take this kindly.

She stretched all five fingers at Chico in the traditional insult and yelled,

'Your mother and your father can come and lick my...'

Chico turned round and returned the compliment.

'Whore!' he shouted at the enraged banku seller.

The woman, a tall and hefty mammy, took a few steps towards the boy, her hand raised.

'You wait for me there!'

But Chico was not going to wait for the onslaught. He quickened his steps and vanished into the night crowd.

'Vulgar woman! If she had been to school, she would not have uttered such filthy words,' he said to himself. But what he had just heard was nothing unfamiliar to him. It was common language in the Bukom neighbourhood. Chico himself had used similar, probably worse, language in the past. Happily, he felt, his repertoire of foul vocabulary was shrinking gradually as a result of his contact with other boys at school-boys who came from homes where all the inmates used flush toilets and soft toilet rolls. Homes where there was civilisation.

He walked towards a kenkey and fish stand. The woman standing behind the smoking kerosene lamp smiled at the approaching boy.

'I want to buy some fish,' Chico announced.

'So Chico, don't you know how to say "good morning"?' the woman asked.

The boy was surprised. People do not normally walk up to a kenkey and fish stand and salute before buying the darn stuff. But then, it was not normal for women standing behind smoking kerosene lamps to call him by his name when he had no idea who they were.

Chico smiled uncomfortably.

'Don't you know me?' the woman asked.

Chico shook his head.

'Of course you should know me. Are you not Ataa Kojo's son?' the woman asked.

'Yes , I am.'

'And you don't know me?'

Chico scratched his head.

'I don't blame you. Your father is so mean he does not bother to show you who his relatives are. When you go home ask him to tell you who Maami Adoley is.'

'He is not at home,' Chico informed her.

'Where has he gone?'

'I don't know.'

'Just like Ataa Kojo. Never at home,' the woman said and brought a sheet of crumpled old newspaper. She removed the polythene covering the kenkey and took one.

'Oh no, I am not buying kenkey. I want to buy some fish ,' the boy quickly explained.

'Oh never mind, take it all the same,' the woman said, and selected some fish and added some pepper. She wrapped the collection neatly in the newspaper and handed the parcel to the waiting boy.

'Tell your father to ask of me sometimes,' she said.

'He is not at home.'

'Well, tell him when he returns.'

'Yes, ma,' Chico replied. He still hesitated, not knowing what to do. The woman noticed the boy's predicament and came to the rescue.

'Good night, Chico,' she said.

'Good night, ma,' he said and walked away.

Chico was completely overwhelmed by the woman's kindness. He never thought that his father had a relative as nice as Maami Adoley. He must find out more about the woman.

The house was still silent when he returned. He was therefore able to eat his dinner in peace. He spread the paper on a table and ate straight from it. He wasted no time on the cold ball and half of kenkey in the kitchen. Maami Adoley's hot kenkey and fish were enough. He drank a cup of water and sighed with satisfaction.

'At least my father has one relative who is civilised,' he said and went to bed.

Chapter 3

When Chico woke up the next morning, his sister Fofo, with whom he shared the same bedroom, was still asleep. He had not noticed her return as he had had a sound sleep himself after a late dinner. He got out of bed, stretched his limbs and pulled on a pair of shorts. He opened the back window and spat out the overnight saliva that had accumulated in his mouth.

'Hey, Fofo!' he called.

'Hmm…hm…who is it?'

'Where did you people go last night?' he asked.

'What?' Fofo was still sleepy.

'I said where did you people go last night?'

'Oh, we went out to celebrate father's birthday,' Fofo said.

'What are you talking about? Since when did father start celebrating his birthday?' Chico asked.

Fofo opened her eyes for the first time.

'Who is talking about father's birthday?' she asked.

'Well , you just did. You said you went out to celebrate father's birthday last night. That's what you said,' her brother reminded her.

'Oh, did I? I mean his…er…his firm presented him with a tiepin.'

'Fofo, what are you talking about? What are you talking about?' he asked again, becoming impatient at the apparent gibberish his sister was talking.

'A tiepin, a gold tiepin.'

'Yes?'

'Father's firm presented him with a gold tiepin,' Fofo said.

'What for?'

'For twenty-five years of loyal service to the firm.'

'So you people went out to booze.'

'Yes, we thought we would go and buy him a drink, you know, just to make him feel good,' Fofo explained.

'And you were so drunk you could not even remove your dress before going to bed.'

Fofo looked at her dress and laughed at the realisation. 'Oh well, I was so tired and sleepy I forgot,' she explained.

'Nobody thinks about me in this house,' Chico grumbled.

'Oh come on, Chico, you know that is not a fair thing to say. You were not in the house. Of course, we would have gone with you,' Fofo said.

But that was not what he meant. He meant the nobody bothered whether he ate or not. 'There was no food in the house and nobody left me any money,' he added.

'But you know where I keep my money. You could have taken some to buy food,' Fofo pointed out.

'Oh yes. The last time I took your money to buy food, you swore at me like a fishwife,' Chico reminded his elder sister and walked out of the room. He washed his face and went into the lavatory.

It was some minutes past seven o'clock. Allotey had just woken up himself but was lying in bed. There was nothing to rush for on a Saturday morning – anyway, since he did not have to go to work. He could take his time and get up when he pleased. He hooked his shirt with his toes and removed it from the back of the chair where he had hung it carelessly the previous night. He removed a half packet of cigarettes and lit one. He blew out rings of smoke and watched them rise and disappear towards the ceiling. Somebody had tuned his radio to the commercial station and he could hear a number he fancied very much.

'Yeah, and I say it again,
Let's go it slow,
Yeah, one more time,
Let's go it slow.'

The chorus sang in response to the rich and soulful voice of Ray Charles.

'Yes, baby, I'm going it slow right here,' Allotey said to himself with a smile. That was what he had wanted. To lie in bed over the weekend and laze about, listening to soulful music; only the music should come from his own wireless set and not from somebody's room in the neighbourhood.

When the song ended, he got up, and with half a stick of his cigarette still left, he made for the toilet. The door was locked from within.

'Who is in there?' he asked.

There was no reply.

'Is that you, Chico?' he asked again.

'Yes,' his younger brother replied from within.

'Well, hurry up!'

Chico was annoyed at this and decided to remain in the place longer than necessary in spite of the stench to which he held a strong objection. Eventually, he came out.

Allotey was still waiting.

'What were you doing in there?' Allotey asked angrily.

'Having a baby,' his younger brother answered simply and walked past him with scorn. He went into his father's room. He did not knock. He had always entered his father's bedroom without knocking and this was one habit he did not intend changing in spite of his exposure to boys from more sophisticated homes.

The oldman was lying in bed, snoring comfortably. The room reeked of strong alcohol. The sight of the sleeping man brought a smile to Chico's face. He went out, shutting the door quietly behind him.

'Hey, Fofo, what did you people do to the old man last night?' he asked his elder sister, when he returned to their room.

'What do you mean?'

'He is still fast asleep, complete with his white suit, shoes and tie on,' he said. They both laughed.

'Well, Chico, I will tell you what happened.'

They had taken the oldman to a bar for some beer. When the drinks were brought, Ataa Kojo would not drink. He said buying him beer was a waste of money and that beer never did him any good. It only upset his stomach and tickled his jaws. What he wanted was the real man's drink. 'Kill Me Quick' was what they should buy for him and not beer. They had asked the barman if he had the stuff. He had. They had always had the stuff since the government legalised it on the market. 'The only sensible thing the government has done,' commented Ataa Kojo.

They had bought him the stuff and he had done justice to it. His spirits had been elevated and they had found an outlet by way of stories which were not altogether clean but were passable, considering that they all were inhabitants of the Bukom neighbourhood.

They had stayed there drinking and laughing at the old man's jokes till the barman had had to tell them to leave, as he had to close.

Fofo continued; 'When we got home, he could hardly walk on his own feet and we had to show him where his room was.'

Chico then asked his sister if she knew of a woman called Maami Adoley.

'The kenkey seller?'

'Yes, she says she is a relative of father's.'

'That is a lie,' Fofo said.

'What do you mean?'

'She is no relative of father's.'

'Well, that's what she told me.'

'And I say she was lying. Where did you meet her anyway?'

'At the square, she was very nice to me.'

'Well, she would be. She happens to be father's girlfriend.' Fofo said.

'What? At his age?' Chico asked.

Fofo laughed. 'Oh Chico, you are a kid indeed. As long as you feel strong enough to want it.'

Chico giggled.

'There was a time when the old man wanted to marry her. That was shortly after our mother's death. Obviously, it had been going on for some time,' Fofo informed her brother.

'Why didn't they get married?'

'She said she wasn't sure if the old man wanted her for her money. Obviously she must have a little hoard somewhere. She has been selling kenkey since I was a little girl and she has no children.'

'I rather like her,' remarked Chico.

'She is a nice woman,' Fofo agreed.

Allotey came into the room and overheard the last sentence.

'Who is a nice woman?' he asked.

'Who is talking to you?' Chico retorted.

'Chico, you are becoming rude these days. If you keep it up, you are not going to get that shirt I promised to buy for you,' Allotey warned.

'Don't bother, brother, you never meant to buy it anyway,' said Chico.

'Well, I have.'

'Lies!'

'It's a fact. It's in my drawer this very minute. Any time you behave better, you can have it,' Allotey said.

Chico's eyes lit up with joy. He dashed out of the room to look for shirt. It would cost him nothing to behave himself, except that he had to make sure.

'Have you really bought it?' Fofo asked when Chico was gone.

'Yes.'

'He will be very happy.'

'Yes, last borns are always lucky. Chico deserves to be happy,' Allotey said.

The rays of the morning streamed through the window and fell on the bed where Ataa Kojo lay. He blinked angrily and finally opened his eyes. They felt sore. He would have liked to shift his position on the bed and sleep some more, but he discovered that something far more compelling had control of the better part of him. He was wickedly hungry. He had missed his usual heavy dinner the previous evening and the excessive alcohol he had consumed instead had left his throat dry.

He got up and staggered into the kitchen. He drank two cups of water before realising that he was still wearing his white suit. He also discovered that he was wearing his shoes, for the pain in his toes was agonizingly insistent. His feet were not used to that particular pair of shoes. They were his ceremonial shoes which he wore only on special occasions; and the last time he wore them was at Karley's wedding some years ago. That was also the last time he wore his white suit. Yes, that was for having such a lovely daughter. That was the day he held his head high and showed the people in the neighbourhood that he, Ataa Kojo, was somebody whose daughter got married in church like the other 'high class' ladies. He had not prayed for nothing. His eldest daughter had got herself a good husband who could help to buy the coffin when he was dead. He would have to keep praying for Fofo too. If only she would come home early from work and stop wearing those ridiculous dresses which left all her thighs exposed, she would perhaps land a man who worked in the Ministries and had his salary paid into the bank. Karley's husband was an agricultural officer and that was just as good. What was important was that folks would not call her Karley again. They would call her 'missus', and she would live in a government bungalow. That was the life for his daughter, several times better than the one she was brought up in.

He could not wish too much for his sons. Boys never usually liked to leave their roots. It would mean paying rent in decent rooms. They would go out and marry no-good girls and bring them home to come and crowd the small family house. Allotey had always said he would move out to a more respected neighbourhood, but he had been saying that for the past two years, ever since he started work. But perhaps that was being too pessimistic. Who knows, the time might come when he would get a big post? Allotey was a good mixer and he was bound to make some friends who had influential friends in the right places. That was how it was done. You had to know somebody who knew somebody. Yes, maybe the time would come when he would have to move into a government bungalow and he, Ataa Kojo, could visit him on Sundays and would be served with iced water from the fridge.

Come to think of it, this was the time for him to start enjoying himself. Chico was no problem to him financially. His two elder brothers could pay his fees, so that he could start thinking of adding another wing to the house. One more bedroom and a proper flush toilet would not be out of place. Yes, he would ask everybody to contribute something at the end of every month for the project. If the boys did not want to leave their roots, then they must make sure that those roots were firm.

He went back into his room and took off his white suit. It had to be washed, ironed and kept for the next occasion. As for the shoes, he would have to pass them on to Allotey or Chico as they were getting too small for his feet.

Ataa Kojo put on his *'mamma'*, he wiggled his aching toes and slipped them into a pair of 'Charlie wotey'. Those rubber slippers were much more comfortable than the confounded shoes. The pains one had to go through to keep up so-called standards and look like the European. Why did he, an African, want to look like a European anyway? Why should he, when the Europeans themselves wanted to look like Africans? Had he not seen many white American tourists walking downtown barefooted and bare-chested when the habit was now extinct even in Bukom?

He came out of his room. 'Now where is everybody?' he called.

'In here.'

He limped into the room where Fofo was still lying in bed and Allotey was sitting at the foot of it, smoking.

'Fofo, why are you still in bed? Are you people not going to work?' the old man asked his children.

'My dear Papa, today happens to be Saturday,' Fofo reminded him.

'Oh, and where is Chico?' he asked again.

'He is in my room,' Allotey replied.

'Hey, Chico, come over here!' the old man shouted. Allotey had noticed his father limping.

'But father, what's wrong with your foot?' he asked.

'Those blasted shoes, they are a complete nuisance. I think they are too small for me now. You can have them if you like,' he said.

'You mean those shoes you had on yesterday?'

'Yes.'

Allotey laughed.

'What is funny? They are good shoes made of pure Moroccan leather. I have had them for years,' Ataa Kojo impressed upon his son

'Exactly, father, you have had them for too long and they are old-fashioned. They are what we call "colo".'

'Nonsense! You children of this generation have no sense in your heads, that is why things are difficult in your time. In my day, you bought a pair of shoes which would last you a lifetime. Now look at the prices you see in the shops; and the articles are not even worth anything. If you don't like it, you can please yourself. Now where is that Chico boy?'

Chico entered the room, wearing a new shirt.

'And where is this shirt coming from?' his father asked.

'From the shops, I guess,' Chico replied.

'Fool, I mean who bought it for you?'

'Allotey bought it for me.' Chico replied.

'Now, this is just what I was saying. Look at that fanciful shirt. Touch it; you would think it was made out of paper. You people do not know what to do with your money. And how much did you pay for it?'

Allotey supplied the information.

'There you are, Tsu!'

'Father, this is what everybody wears in town these days,' Chico said. 'And so it came to pass that in a whole town of crazy people, the only sane one is my father,' Chico joked.

'Will you shut your mouth? I should ask why you came home so late from school yesterday.'

Chico explain that he had to hold a meeting after classes. Then he had stayed on to play some table tennis.

His explanation passed without comment, but deep down, the old man was beginning to nurse some pride that Chico had been thought good enough. He was careful not to show this openly, for the little boy might get big-headed, and also the others might become jealous for they never got themselves elected secretaries when they were at school.

'Fofo, you'd better see and organise some breakfast, I am hungry,' Ataa Kojo instructed his daughter.

'You must be, the way you drank last night.'

'Ha, ha, that was something. You kids made me feel really good last night. You must do that often. God, I was so drunk I slept in my suit. That reminds me, Chico, you go and wash it and iron it neatly. You had better do it now before you vanish from the house.'

'Yes, father,' Chico said and made for the door.

'Chico!' Allotey called.

'You have not thanked me for the shirt.'

Chico smiled and said: 'Thank you very much, brother.' He went out.

Chapter 4

The wind of change had been blowing across the earth's surface for centuries before someone made headlines with the phrase. This wind had been affecting nations, peoples, their attitudes and their ways of thinking – sometimes for the worse, and sometimes, too, for the better. Perhaps this is humanly understandable because, after all, 'For better or for worse' is used freely in churches. Perhaps also, one might justifiably say that this explains why the human race tends to be caught with its pants down in the matter of development – sometimes very positive, but all too often, far too negative.

In every city, there is one area which remains defiantly and stubbornly averse to change or development. One such area in the municipality of Accra is James Town, with Bukom as its centre – the epitome of the black neighbourhood of the old order.

A cross-section of the inhabitants of this area would reveal that they are principally fishermen or of fisherman stock.

Perhaps the only important visible changes which have been brought about by progressive development are the disappearance of the old dusty roads, which are now replaced by tarred ones, a few more elementary schools and smattering of traffic lights.

These are some of the obvious changes that are readily recognisable by non-inhabitants of James Town. But to the inmates of the area themselves, the principal difference that modern development has made to the area is the absence of the Ga Mantse. His Excellency used to live in the midst of his subjects. But now, times have changed and he has had to move house. He had moved into a more dignified palace designed by an architect, furnished with all the modern trappings and situated far in the suburbs of the municipality, several miles away from the old palace.

The well-kept lawns, the driveways and the solid iron gates make it a far cry from the old structure. That is as it should be. The Mantse of Ghana's capital must live in a palace befitting his position. After all, there were still lesser chiefs in James Town to cope with minor matters. What was more, the Nii Wulomo had not moved house. Fetish priests don't move house like that.

But one man who viewed the Ga Mants's new palace with displeasure was Ataa Kojo. Not because he contributed in any way towards the building or any such thing. When the Mantse We palace was in James Town, he had paid regular visits to the place. The distance was not that far and he would walk it in minutes to see an old boyhood friend who was now one of the chief's linguists.

He had always looked forward to these weekend visits because it promised generous offerings of drinks, and food from the chief's own kitchen.

But now, he could not keep up with these habits. The palace was now too far away for him to be able to walk the distance; paying taxi fares was not one the things he fancied much. If he had that money to pay for a taxi, he would rather walk across the road, buy himself some 'Kill Me Quick' and listen to dirty stories from the drunken palates of his friends.

It was a particularly hot day, which was propitious for a swim in the sea. There had not been much to do these Saturday afternoons now that nobody went to work. He had always gone for a dip in the sea on Saturday afternoons anyway, a habit he had acquired since his younthful days and which he knew was good for his bones. Besides, there were always the fisher-folks there to chat with. He knew their ways; he even knew how to mend a fishing net. His old man had been a fisherman himself and he had often gone fishing with him when he was a lad.

'Hey, Ataa Kojo, come, come,' an old friend shouted.

'Go away!'

'Look at the fool. I said come here!'

'You got something for me?'

'Nonsense, I want you to give us a hand at mending this net.'

'How much do I get?'

'Fish. 'What else?'

'So if I don't help you mend the goddam net, you won't give me fish?'

'Nonsense. Don't you know that hand go hand come?'

'As for you, you have the brains of an octopus.'

There was general laughter.

Ataa Kojo took one end of the net and started to work. His deft fingers moved efficiently to and fro to the admiration of his old mate.

'You know, Ataa Kojo, you should have been a fisherman.'

'Foolish, do I look like a fisherman? Don't you know I am a government worker?' he retorted.

This brought laughter from the other man. He knew that working with the government had not made Ataa Kojo any better than himself.

But Ataa Kojo was proud of himself without despising his friend. His own father had been a fisherman. But he had not chosen to follow in his footsteps. Instead, he had joined the King's army and had saluted the British flag, sung 'God save the King' and had even fought in a war he did not understand. He had not complained. In fact, he had liked it, because it had meant regular pay, better accommodation at the army barracks and a supply of black boots and shinning buttons. But now all that was over. Nobody saluted the whitemen's flag or sang 'God Save the King' or fought the wars of the colonial masters any more.

Independence had changed all that. Kwame Nkrumah had said it was better to be independent. We are doing our own thing, whether rightly or wrongly. That man was right. It was better to see a black man in the Osu Castle. A black man can also ride in a big black car with policemen escorting him on horses and motor cycles. It did not matter if he, Ataa Kojo could not ride in one of those things himself. Everybody could not possibly sit in a big car or live in the Castle. All men were not born to be the same. God himself created the world that way, and God was no fool. It was not a mistake that some fingers on the same hand are longer than others.

'Hey, Ataa Kojo, what are you going to do for Christmas?'

'Huh?'

'Are you going to kill a goat?'

'What's wrong with fish?'

'At least you must buy some biscuits.'

'Oh yes, that I will buy.'

The dialogue was not in fact out of place, for Christmas was almost at hand. The shops had started decorating their windows with toys and drinks. And in the streets and markets, bells were perpetually ringing announcing Christmas items for sale. The sound of these bells could be heard almost everywhere as hawkers peddled their items. And on that afternoon, one such bell was ringing out loud in the area where Ataa Kojo and his friend were mending their fishing nets.

'Hey, small boy, come here!' Ataa Kojo hailed the boy ringing the bell.

'What are you selling?'

'These.'

'What are they?'

'Toilet rolls.'

'What are they used for?'

The boy told him

'Who sent you?'

'My mother asked me to sell them,' the boy explained.

'Does your mother use them herself?'

'No.'

'What does she use?' Ataa Kojo asked.

'Newspaper,' the boy replied.

'And what's wrong with me using newspaper myself, ha?'

'Well, big people use this one.'

'Have you seen any big people living in this area?'

'No.'

'Well, then, get the hell out of here and stop ringing that bell!' Ataa Kojo shouted at the boy. The poor boy hurried away.

'Foolish, I thought he was selling biscuits,' Ataa Kojo said.

'Ataa Kojo, you shame us,' one of the fishermen said.

'Me?'

'Yes, you really shame us.'

'Now what sort of talk is that? Me shame you? How?' demanded Ataa Kojo.

'After working with the whiteman firm all these years, you never learnt how to use toilet roll?'

'Nonsense. As for you, only nonsense ever comes out of that mouth of yours. What has working with the whiteman got to do with using toilet rolls?'

In reply, Ataa Kojo got a burst of laughter from his fisherman friends.

'Foolish, why should I spend money on toilet roll when an old newspaper can do the same thing?' Ataa Kojo wanted to know.

One of the fishermen pointed out that Ataa Kojo was a scholar and that only the previous Friday they had seen him walking down the street and word had reached them that the whiteman had given him a gold tiepin.

Ataa Kojo smiled with pride and said, 'Well, that's true. Not all people get tiepins presented to them. But then that does not make me any different enough to spend good money on silly things like toilet rolls. Now if you folks are going to annoy me, I am going to stop mending the net. Here I am helping you yet you will not keep your big mouths shut.' His friends laughed, but did not pursue the teasing. They knew that Ataa Kojo was a jolly good chum, but he was a chum who would walk out on them if they tried to make fun of a thing he held dear to his heart.

Mending of the net resumed in earnest and one of the men broke into a song. Obviously, the song was inspired by the approach of a young woman who had just emerged from the public bathrooms. She had a bucket in her hand and had only one piece of cloth on her. She was mopping traces of water still trickling down from her hair.

'Akweley came out of the water
She was wet.
Wet all outside.
I made her dry up
Before making her wet again.
Akweley will now go into the water again
She will be wet.
Wet all outside.'

The young woman heard the song. She had heard it before but she knew that it was being sung at the particular moment for her benefit.

'Tsu! Nonsense doings!' she hurled the insult at the men and quickened her steps, shaking her behind with maximum agility.

The men burst into laughter at this. 'Oh my, that girl has something. I will not kick a thing like that out of my bed,' Ataa Kojo said with a laugh.

'Especially when she is dry and powdered and smelling nice,'

'Yeah!' agreed Ataa Kojo.

'Ah, but, Ataa Kojo, you wouldn't do a thing like that,' said one of the men.

'And why not?' he asked.

'Because you wouldn't jump into bed with your own daughter. And your Fofo is about the same age as that girl.

'Nonsense, man. That girl may be the same age as my daughter, but she is not my daughter,' explained Ataa Kojo.

'I tell you, that daughter of yours might be giving what she has to a man as old as you. That's what they do these days,' one of the men said.

'I don't want to think about that. She is a woman,' Ataa Kojo said.

Chapter 5

Ataa Kojo was right. For back in the house, Fofo had just come out of the bathroom and was in the middle of powdering and applying her feminine toiletries to her body. She was standing in front of the tall mirror and making sure that every bit of the application got to where it was meant to go. Halfway through, she stopped, looking at herself in the mirror. Then girlishly, she let the piece of cloth wrapped about her drop to the ground. Thus, standing naked before the mirror, she stared steadily at what she saw. Then slowly and with a deliberate ballet move, she made a quarter turn to the right, stretching up her spine and pushing out her young firm breasts. She held that posture for a few seconds before relaxing with a smile. It was a smile of satisfaction, the satisfaction of a woman pleased that she has what it takes to make a woman.

'Ha, a million men will give an eye to sleep with me. Ha!' She smiled again and ran her hands caressing down the contours of her anatomy. There was something missing. But what was it? 'Ah yes, the beads. Some men like them. I hear they like to play with them. Such nonsense! Why should a man play with my beads? Why should I allow a man to play with the beads around my waist?' She put her hands on her waist. 'Maybe I look better without those beads, or do I?'

She picked up the two strings of beads and put them on. She examined the result in the mirror.

'No, its better without. That is what nature meant it to be. I was not born with beads on. Any man who wants to sleep with me will have to do that without the business of playing with the beads.'

She had not thought of who that man would be. She had not slept with any yet and she need not make up her mind whom she would sleep with yet. There were two men she had been seeing for some time.

First, there was Mr Appiah in the office. He was about the age of her father, or almost. A nice man indeed who had been buying her lunch and pinching her bottom in the office each time he called her to explain an error in her typing. She had known all along that he would like to sleep with her but he had not said so. And there was Lawrence. Lawrence had been a clerk in the shop she had worked in when she was a sales girl. But he had not given any indication of his intentions.

She had been persuaded by her colleagues to go to night classes for shorthand and typing. Then she had studied and qualified. She had changed jobs for the present one in a government department. Then one day, she had run in to Lawrence at the bus stop. That was when Lawrence started his advances. Nice boy Lawrence.

'Lawrence and Mr Appiah want to sleep with me, ha! They will have to wait till I make up my mind. And when I do, it will be without beads. I want it natural and complete. No side activities like playing with beads or such silly things.'

She cupped both breasts in her hands, slightly propping them as if to weigh them. She liked the feel. The weight was also right. She burst out laughing and picked up the powder to apply more to the underparts.

The laughter brought Chico into the room. He found his elder sister standing in front of the mirror in the nude.

'Aw, Fofo!'

'Get out!' she said, without any attempt to cover up.

'Why do you always spend so much time standing in front of the mirror naked like that?' asked Chico.

'Does that bother you?'

'It revolts me,' said Chico.

'Liar! You wish you could have it.'

'S'pose I was not your sister, would you not want to sleep with me?' Fofo asked.

'Ha! What do you think you've got that will make a man sleep with you? I have seen women who have better things than what you've got, yet they don't spend hours before the mirror looking at themselves,' Chico said with a sneer.

The remarks shocked Fofo out of her girlish stupor. For a few seconds, she stood still. When she recovered, she picked up the cloth from the floor and covered herself. She walked slowly to her younger brother.

'Chico, have you slept with a woman already?'

Chico's lips moved as if to speak, but the words never came out. His elder sister was still standing before him, her eyes searching and waiting for her kid brother to speak. He did not speak.

'Chico, I asked you a question.'

'Hmm?'

'Have you ever slept with a woman?' Fofo repeated the question, still keeping her eyes on her brother. Chico's face did not give anything away; and if his sister wanted to know what she wanted to know, the information would have to come from his voice and not his face. And he was not going to speak, not until he knew his voice could not give him away.

Chico shook his head.

'Liar!' Fofo accused.

Chico moved away from his sister's searching eyes questioning him for an answer.

'Chico, don't run away,' Fofo said.

'I' m not running away.'

'Come and sit down,' she said, took her brother's hand and sat him on the bed. She was now convinced that her brother had slept with a woman. At first, this awareness had come to her as a shock, but now it was one of curiosity. How could her little brother, at such a tender age, have come into close contact with a naked woman and experienced what she, much older as she was, had not experienced?

'Tell me about her,' she pleaded.

'About who?'

'The woman.'

'She is not old.'

'How old is she?'

'I don't know.'

'Do you sleep with her often?'

'No.'

'How often?'

'Oh Fofo!'

'Please, brother Chico, I want to know. Tell me about it.' Fofo pleaded. But Chico was neither going to tell his big sister about HER nor about IT. It had been a very memorable experience. It had been a fleeting encounter, but every stage of it had remained vivid in his mind.

'Chico!'

'Yes?'

'Tell me,' she pleaded again, this time taking her brother's shoulders in her hands and shaking him frantically. But Chico's mind was far away. He was staring at his sister's face in a daze, and in her eyes, he could see the whole incident.

They had gone to Cape Coast for friendly sports meeting with a girls secondary school. The four-day meeting had included table tennis and Chico had won his tournament comfortably over his female opponent.

The girl had refused to shake hands after the contest and had turned away angrily from her victor's outstretched hand. This had met the disapproval of students from both schools as unsportmanlike. Chico, on the other hand, had been embarrassed and rueful. Perhaps, he should have known better and allowed the girl to win the match. But nobody had told him the principles of good manners when playing table tennis with a female opponent. He had gone all out and smashed and balled his fast back strokes so that the girl had had no answer. And in attempt to save one of these wicked strokes, the girl had slipped and had fallen down revealing her pink panties. This had humiliated the girl who had flashed a pair of angry eyes at her tormentor before picking herself up.

That evening, all the students were given permission to go to town and see a play which another college was staging. Just before the bus came to pick the students up, the captain of the visiting team, Emmanuel Addo, also a boy from the Bukom neighbourhood, came running up.

'Chico, you going to see the play?' he asked.

'Yes.'

'We are going to the movies. Do you want to come along?'

'Yes. But who are you going with? Chico wanted to know.

'Don't you know I have girl in this school?'

'No.'

'Well, I have, and we have decided to go to the pictures instead. Find yourself a girl and come along if you like.'

Chico would have liked that, but then he had no girl and he did not know how to find one.

'Chico, don't look now but your girl is coming,' Addo said.

'Which one?'

'The girl you floored this afternoon at the tournament.'

Chico could not help turning. His eyes met the girl's. She was possibly going to wait for the bus. As soon as she saw Chico, she turned her eyes in the other direction.

Chico's heart beat faster.

'Call her, Chico,' Addo encouraged.

'I don't know her name.'

'Doesn't matter, just call her.'

'I said I don't know her name.'

'Psstt, excuse me!' Addo called.

The girl stopped and turned towards the two.

'Go on Chico,' Addo whispered.

'Er... Excuse me,' Chico said.

'What?' the girl asked sharply, standing her ground.

'Go and invite her to the movies,' Addo encouraged his friend again.

Chico cleared his throat and moved towards the girl.

'Good evening. My name is Chico.'

'I know that,' the girl said. It was not surprising because all the boys kept shouting his name throughout the contest.

But the thought that the girl knew his name boosted his morale.

'Well...er... I wanted to say I'm sorry.'

'For what?'

'This afternoon.'

The girl said nothing.

'If we meet again, I will let you win,' Chico promised.

The girl's face softened. The anger faded away but she still did not speak.

'I thought I was playing against a boy,' Chico said.

'Do I look like a boy?' asked the girl.

'No, no, I don't mean that. It's just that I always play with boys back at our school.'

'You have not played with a girl before?'

'No.'

'You did this afternoon,' the girl said.

'Yes, of course, I should have known better than to put you through all that. Let me say I was embarrassed when you fell down and everybody looked.

The girl laughed.

'They did not see anything,' she said.

'I saw something.'

'What?'

'It was pink.'

'That's not what I meant,' the girl said. But Chico knew what she meant and he was not going to mention it. It was a subject he had never discussed with any woman. It was fun discussing it with boys but how do you go about a thing like that with a girl?

The bus arrived and the students began hurrying towards it.

'You going to see the play?' Chico asked.

'Yes!'

'We are going to the movies. Why don't you come along?' Chico suggested.

'Oh but…' Addo cut in, calling Chico. He was walking with one of the students from the girl's school, a smallish girl with extra features.

'Chico, are you coming?'

'Yes.'

'But…'began Chico's companion.

'It's all right. Let's go together. I hear the picture is good.'

'Well…'

'C'mon, let's go. We go by the bus to town and walk the rest, Addo said and started moving with his girlfriend. Chico and his companion hesitated.

'Let's go.' When they got to the cinema, there was no sign of activity. An enquiry revealed that there had been a power failure and therefore there was not going to be any cinema show.

'Dammit,' Addo swore. He then suggested that they should go for walk.

'Where?'

'The beach is just a few yards away.'

'Let's go to see the play.

'It must be half-way through now and we shall not follow the story.'

'Let's go back to the compound.'

'They will ask where we've been.'

'So what do we do?'

'The beach is only a few yards away.'

'All right.'

So they went to the beach.

There were no stars in the sky and the moon was perpetually dodging behind the clouds. All they could see were the tall coconut trees in silhouette.

Addo and his girlfriend walked hand-in-hand and away from Chico and his companion.

Because visibility was almost nil, they could not see them, only hear the voices. After some minutes, Chico could not hear their voices again.

'Where are they now?' Chico's companion asked.

'Over there.'

'I can't hear their voices anymore.'

'Addo!' Chico called.

There was no reply.

'Let's go and find out,' Chico said and took the girl by the hand.

They found Addo and his girlfriend lying on Addo's college blazer, spread out in the sand. His trousers were lying close by.

Chico and his companion stopped, watching the two bodies in one close unit.

Chico turned to look at the girl next to him. The girl heaved a sharp sigh.

Chico released his hand from the girl's and slowly took his blazer and spread it on the ground. Slowly, he took the girl in his arms and gently lowered her on to the ground. The girl did not resist.

Chico's hands began to work down the girl till they touched her underwear.

'Are they pink?' he asked.

'Take a look for yourself.'

But Chico could not discern the colour in the dark. He felt his way.

The memory of that incident, the breaking-in, brought a smile to Chico's face. It was the smile of re-living an experience in discovery of immense fascination.

'Who was she, Chico?' his sister asked the question, this time more of a plea.

Chico laughed loudly. 'I don't know what you are talking about. Who said I have slept with a woman?'

'Nobody has said that, but I know you have.'

'Tha's not true.'

'I won't tell anybody. You can trust me.'

Trust! How could he trust anybody with an experience like that? It was meant to be secret and intimate. Otherwise, folks would be doing it in the streets, like the dogs do at Bukom. Besides, there was nothing to boast about – it's a natural thing to do. If it were not natural, that girl would have resisted and kept her pants on tight. But even the girl, who owned the better part of the union, felt it was natural to give. God created it that way. The study of anatomy showed that, and the Bible has proved that God is the creator of the human body.

But even looking at the whole incident in retrospect, he wasn't quite sure whether it was worth all the fuss people make about it. Perhaps it was the experience, and the excitement at the thought of burying oneself inside a woman and perhaps also the enjoyment of reliving an intimate communion with a woman.

'Chico, you are bad boy,' Fofo finally pronounced, now convinced, without any trace of doubt, that her kid brother had 'discovered' what she had not yet tasted.

'Tsu!' Chico said and walked out of the room. Fofo remained seated on the bed for a long time, a maze of confusion. How could Chico go and do a thing like that? Bad boy, going to sleep with a woman! Why, the little brat thinks he is a big man.

She got up and continued powdering herself. This time, she did not want to stand in front of the mirror.

As a woman, there was more she could do, or could have done to her.

Somebody must see her as a woman and want to open her to a new discovery, a discovery which even her little brother thought was nothing to bother about. She ought to be ashamed of herself, still a virgin at her age. Ah, Chico is bad. Wait! I will show him!

She finished powdering and pulled on her cotton pants. She changed her mind and dived into the bottom drawer of the dressing table and fished out a nylon pair. It was a pair she had bought last year but had never dared to put on. They were too transparent and when she had tried them on and stood before the mirror, she could see practically everything. 'Ah, this is obscene,' she had said and buried the pants in the bottom drawer. But now, looking at them, they did not look vulgar. Why, they were attractive. She put them on.

'Yes, that's it. Any man seeing me in panties like this will blaze with desire.'

But the question that hit her was how a man could see those panties. Girls do not parade the streets wearing only panties. Something has to happen. Perhaps the wind would have to blow real hard to lift the dress before bystanders can see. Or you would have to sit real vulgar to reveal your underwear-a thing she would never dream of doing. Makes a girl look cheap and common. And, although she had been born and bread in James Town , she had good manners and she intended to be regarded as a lady. After all, most of the great ladies in Accra had James Town blood in them.

Mrs Dunae was born in James Town of a fisherman's family and had had very little education, but she had been married to Mr Dunae of the Senior Civil Service, who had had her improved, and her plain fisher language cleaned up. Even she would not sit down and deliberately reveal her panties, not even to attract the Duke of Edinburgh.

But why did she have to bother her little head about things like that? If a man was destined to see a woman's underwear, he would. All she had to worry about was how to make it natural. A man would have to discover her one day anyway and that man would have to dispose of the underwear first.

Yes, the man would have to remove it himself – she was not going to make herself easy to reach by removing all the obstacles. Man was made to sweat. Yes, man was made to sweat. And she was going to let the first man sweat his guts out. Ha, that first man was going to be a lucky man having a virgin like her. He would be having fun and total satisfaction while she would be having only a little fun mixed with the pain of first experience. Her friends had told her that the first experience was sometimes painful and could even reduce one to tears. But it was nothing to run away from. Once you were created a woman, you had to go through it, just like having a baby. Sometimes if a woman was unlucky, she would bleed. But blood was nothing for a woman to be scared of. Why, she saw the darn stuff every month. One of a dozen things a woman, a normal woman, had to live with.

'Ha, God must be a funny man, a really funny man to create all that for a woman, just to make her normal. If only He knew how much annoyance they cause women. Anyway, it's not surprising. God himself is a man. That's just like men. They don't give a fig about women. They would sleep with you, make you pregnant. And when you are heavy with child and spitting and vomiting first thing in the morning, they would be taking it easy and looking around for another woman to sleep with. Funny people, men. Funny man, God.

She dressed up, ready to go out. She had been invited to an afternoon dance. She knew that the boy had been trying very hard for months and she knew what he wanted. Perhaps this was the time to give him what he wanted. She would make it worth the trouble and the long wait. It would also be a good chance to discover the expected unknown. He would have to be gentle about it. She had heard how some boys were rough and crude.

Fofo took a final look at herself in the mirror and was satisfied that she looked presentable and that nothing that was not meant to be shown was showing.

Just as she was ready to leave the room, she heard her father's voice barking out side.

'Where is everybody?'

'I'm here.'

'Where?' Ataa Kojo demanded.

'In my room,' Fofo replied.

'Well come out,' the father ordered.

She came out.

Ataa Kojo took a long look at his daughter. 'Do you go to work on Saturdays?' he asked with a trace of annoyance.

'No.'

'Then what are you dressed up like that for?'

'Going out.'

'Well, I brought some fish from the seaside. You'd better peel off that silly dress and cook something for me to eat.'

Fofo did not react. She just stood there.

Chico came out of his father's room then. 'Oh,' he said when he saw the scene. There was his elder sister dressed up and standing before Ataa Kojo who was holding a netting sac containing fresh fish and both of them staring at each other saying nothing.

'Fofo, did you hear what I said?' the father demanded angrily.

'Well, let Chico cook the food for a change. If he is big enough to sleep with women, he must be able to cook, shit!' Fofo said and stormed out of the house.

Ataa Kojo turned slowly to his son. 'What, Chico! Did I hear right?'

'Lies, all lies, I swear!' Chico protested.

Fofo had a half dozen reasons for not hailing a taxi as soon as she got outside the home, and although a couple of taxis slowed down on seeing her, she ignored them and walked on. For one thing, although she had said she was going out, she had no particular place in mind. Usually those who saw her dressed up like that on Saturday afternoon would automatically conclude that she was going to a teatime dance.

Teatime dances were where most youngsters went on Saturday afternoons. The gate fees were cheaper and you could attend one and return home before your parents began to miss you. But then Fofo was not the girl to walk into one alone. Folks would think she had come to get herself picked up. The truth, however, was that it was at these dances that young women met young men, but then the circumstances had to be forgotten. One did not have to make it look obvious. The boys could go on their own and no one would complain or suspect their intentions.

'Eei, Fofo, where are you going to, all dressed up like a lady?' an elderly woman in the neighbourhood asked.

'Well, perhaps you don't know that I am a lady,' Fofo replied with a touch of sneer in her voice.

'Oh, I'm sorry, lady. I know you are a lady. I was only trying to say that I like your dress, that's all.

Fofo's attitude changed. A slow, reluctant smile played on her lips.

'I was only joking. Actually, I am going to see a friend at Cantonments,' she said. It was a lie because she knew nobody at Cantonments and she had only mentioned it because she knew that people living in that area belonged to the upper class and she, educated as she was and working in a government office, was associated with that class. She must not be taken lightly.

'Yoo, don't be long.' the woman said.

When Fofo was out of earshot, she said, 'These women and their big mouths. They only have to see me in a good dress and they start the gossip.'

What she did not hear was what the woman said when she was out of earshot. 'Now this Fofo girl is getting big for her shoes. She thinks she is the only girl who is educated in this neighbourhood. Wait till she gets into trouble. We shall all smell it.'

This expectation was not unknown to Fofo. Most of the girls who had been educated and had been loud about it in the neighbourhood had got pregnant without proper customary marriage. This would generate a lot of gossip and speculation as to who did it. Women would talk about if for nine months and two weeks; and when the baby was born, they would make sure they attended the naming ceremony to see whom the baby resembled and who the father really was.

But Fofo was not going to give anybody a chance. She was going to be very careful about these things and even when she got laid, it would be under strict safety measures and no nonsense about it.

After walking for about two hundred yards, she felt she would either have to join a bus or take a taxi.

She joined the queue at the next bus stop. Half an hour later, a bus came. It could only take four people and Fofo was among that lucky four.

A man who was also in the queue but could not board the bus, walked up to Fofo and asked her where she was going .

'Adabraka,' she replied.

'Well, I am going to Adabraka too. So why don't you let us take a taxi and share the fare?' the man suggested.

Fofo agreed, but with reluctance. Nothing to be afraid of. The man could not force her to go along with him, if she did not want to – not in broad daylight.

They got a taxi and jumped into it.

'Where are you going to?' the driver asked.

'Adabraka,' Fofo and the man replied in unison.

The man then asked Fofo which part of Adabraka she was going to.

'Near the market.'

'Same area,' the man said.

'Oh?'

'Teatime,' he said.

'So?'

'Yes – I thought that was where you were going.'

'No, actually, I am going to see a friend of mine,' Fofo informed him.

'I see.'

They did not speak again until they got to Adabraka.

'This friend of yours…' the man began.

'Yes,…?'

'Is he taking you to a teatime?'

'She is a girl,' Fofo corrected.

'Oh, I see Errr…in that case, why don't you come together to the dance?'

'What?'

'Well, ask her to come along. I will take you, with me, it doesn't matter if I don't know you. It takes a day to know somebody, like they say.'

Fofo smiled. She knew what the man was up to but she was on her guard.

'Well… what do you say?' the man pressed his suggestion.

'Hmm… the thing is, I don't know if my friend will be persuaded.'

'Then ask her.'

'So?'

'Yes.'

'Hmm…all right.'

The taxi driver followed Fofo's direction to her friend's house. She was at home.

The man paid off the taxi driver and waited outside the house.

'Hey, Grace, guess the adventure I ran into on my way here,' she said.

'What happened?' Grace asked.

Fofo told her the whole story.

'Really, so where is he?'

'Outside.'

'So?'

'Yes.'

'Oh, you're kidding.'

'True, true, I swear.'

'Let me see,' Grace said and went into her room to peep at the man through the curtained window. 'Hey! Its true,' she said when she returned.

'Well, what do you think?' Fofo asked.

'Do you want to go?' Grace asked.

'I don't know, do you?'

Grace said she did not mind and since they had nothing to do and the dance would cost them nothing, they might as well go.

'So what do I tell him?'

'Tell him to wait,' Grace advised.

'Outside?'

'Well, we cannot bring him here to come and sit down. Besides, when I finish with my bath, I would have to dress up with him sitting in the room.'

'I am sure he wouldn't mind that,' Fofo said.

The two girls burst out laughing.

'All right, I will go and tell him to come back in half an hour,' Fofo suggested.

'Yes, yes, you go and tell him that,' Grace said and rushed into the bathroom.

Fofo was polite about it. She told the man that she had managed to convince her friend but then since women took time to get ready, she would ask him to come back, please, in half an hour.

The man agreed. It was better than the prospect of going to a dance with no assurance of a dance. But if he walked into the place, flanked on either side by a dame, people were going to see what a guy he was. And damn the expense, he would get his pay packet next week anyway.

The bath was a quick one and when Grace joined her friend in the room she said: 'Hey! Fofo, you do know that this man is not taking us to the dance just for the fun of it?'

'What?'

'Ha, ha, as for you. But did you think you were going to drink the poor man's beer and go free?'

'Well, I did not ask for it. He offered to take me. Besides, he might turn out to be a nice man.'

'Sure as hell, girl. All men are nice.' Grace said she was speaking from experience. But then she had consoled herself for some of the things a woman had to go through. The first man a girl meets was not necessarily destined to be the right one so what could one do? She laughed and turned to her friend.

'Well, I don't want to frighten you. You are already suspicious about men and I think it is the right thing to do. Every man is nice to a woman and that includes those who want to jump into bed with you. All you have to do is make sure they do not get you cheap.

'Well, no man has ever had me yet.'

'I know that,' Grace said.

'You think that is not good, don't you?'

'Well, I don't really know. This can go on for a quite some time, and before you know what, you are even afraid of men. One of my aunts used to be like that,' said Grace.

She did not know that her friend had made up her mind to discover and be discovered. She would not be outdone by her kid brother. But, as she had said, it had to be under strict safety conditions.

They chatted about dresses as Grace powdered up and dressed. But as she put her shoes on, there was a knock on the door.

'Christ, this man is really in a hurry.'

The knock was repeated.

'Who is it?'

'It's me, Kofi,' a male voice answered.

Grace recognised her boyfriend's voice.

'Come in, Kofi.'

Kofi entered the room. He stopped in his tracks when he saw Grace dressed to go out.

'Hey, Gracie, where do you think you are going?' Kofi asked.

'Teatime,' she answered simply.

'With whom?'

'Fofo.'

'Who else?'

'A man.'

'What man?' Kofi asked angrily.

Just then there was another knock on the door.

'Fofo, it must be half an hour now?' Grace asked her friend meaningfully.

'It must be.'

The knock was repeated.

'Yes, come in.'

The man came in, but he stopped on seeing Kofi.

'Oh, we are ready. This is my friend Grace and this is Kofi.'

Fofo made a casual introduction. She was wise not to attempt to introduce the man because she did not know his name.

'I'm Kweku Ampoma,' the man introduced himself.

Grace put a final touch to her lipstick and turned to Kofi.

'Kofi, are you ready to go too?'

'Grace, I' m going to murder you one of these days,' Kofi threatened.

'I know, that's why I'm going to be very much dead one of these days. Shall we go?'

They all walked out of the room.

Chapter 6

The band had just finished playing its signature tune when the group arrived. The teatime dance had just started and there was no rush to go on the floor. The band itself, seven-piece outfit, had not even warmed up their instruments. One of their members had not arrived yet and there was hope that he would come in due course. The proprietor of the club, a short and sinewy man emerged, glanced at his watch and approached the bandleader.

'Look, man, when are you going to start playing?' he asked angrily.

'We have started, boo,' the leader replied with a smile.

'I haven't heard anything.'

'We have just played our signature tune.'

'What?' The proprietor didn't understand.

'Our signature tune, we have just played it, boo.'

'Well, I don't want any signature, I want you to play some music and let the kids dance. It cost me good money to hire you boys, you know,' the proprietor reminded him.

'So?'

'I say play some music, do you hear me?'

'Yeah, man, yeah!' the leader said and turned to his boys. The latecomer had still not arrived, but it did not matter. They could play something to let the kids dance.

'All right, boys, let's go. Onipa – one, two, three…'

The band swung into a tuneful high life number. Fofo and her party had found themselves a table and ordered their drinks. The band played on but none of the people around made any effort to go onto the dance floor. This did not worry the band boys. Theirs was to play and get paid for it. And in any case, that was the usual thing at afternoon dance sessions. The dancers would only move onto the floor when they had had a few beers in their bellies to help break down their inhibitions.

The missing bandsman arrived. He was neatly dressed in a pair of navy blue trousers, black shoes and white socks, and a rather loud reddish shirt. He grinned broadly and stepped on the bandstand. He dislodged his guitar from its casing, plugged the lead in the amplifier and sat down to plug the strings. The chords he plucked on the guitar were woefully out of tune. The band leader turned on him angrily. 'Stop it! Shit, man, don't you see you are playing discord?' The offending guitarist grinned broadly and stopped playing. He started fidgeting. He pulled out a crumpled cigarette from his breast pocket and started looking into his trouser pockets for matches. He did not find any so he stuck the crumpled cigarette back into his breast pocket and started snapping his fingers to the rhythm of the music.

When the music ended, the leader of the band called him to attention.

'Look, Sammy, I'm going to sack you from the band,' he threatened.

'Chief, please, it was not my fault,' Sammy offered what he thought could be an ample explanation for all that he must have done wrong.

'You wait and see. You wait and see. You'd better tune your fucking guitar before you play it.'

'Okay, chief,' Sammy obeyed. And with the help of the saxophonist, he tuned his guitar to a tolerable standard. The club was filling up and the chatter around the tables was becoming louder and heartier.

At Fofo's group's table, everybody was drinking beer, except Grace.

'Grace, that is going to be your last gin and lime, so you'd better go easy on it,' her boyfriend warned.

'Really, Kofi, you can be difficult sometimes. What is gin and lime to you?'

'It's nothing to me, that's why I'm no more buying large tots for you. It's more expensive than the beer. And I don't see what's wrong with beer anyway,' Kofi complained.

'Oh Kofi, I don't know what you are going on about. Its all right if you don't want to buy me a drink. If you won't buy it, then don't bother. I'm sure I will get a nice man around this place to buy me gin and lime,' Grace said in a tone which was unmistakably a threat.

'Grace, I'm going to murder you one of these days.'

'You're jealous,' Grace accused.

'Nonsense!'

'Shame.'

'Foolish!'

'Hoo, you're jealous.'

'Look Grace, if you annoy me, I'll get up and go,' Kofi threatened.

Grace laughed.

Kofi got up and stormed out of the club.

'Let him go,' Grace said.

'No, Grace, you were not fair. You really annoyed him. I'm sure he was only joking about the gin and lime,' Fofo said.

'Well, I was also joking. I think you should go and call him back,' the man said.

'No, I won't.'

'Oh Grace, please.'

'Oh …well.' Grace said and left the club.

Her departure was a welcome thing for the man. He leaned forward to fill up Fofo's glass. He did not lean back after it. Instead, he looked Fofo straight in the eyes. To divert her eyes from the stranger's searching gaze, she picked up her glass and sipped.

'Ha, Grace is a funny girl,' she said.

'I think Fofo is an interesting girl,' the man said.

'Who, me?'

'Yes.'

'How?'

'You don't seem to talk much,' the man said.

'Well, that should make me uninteresting, don't you think so?' Fofo asked.

'No, that's not what I mean.'

'What do you mean then?'

'I mean I like you ,' the man said and Fofo laughed.

'Is that funny?' he asked.

'What?'

'What I said.'

'Oh no, it was not funny.'

'But you laughed.'

'Yes, must I not laugh?' Fofo queried.

'Please do.'

'No, I will not,' she said, sipped her beer again and smiled. The man smiled back and sipped his beer.

The band started playing again. This time it was a rock number and the singer was screaming like a lunatic in his attempt to sound like the singer on the gramophone record. The result was not very pleasant to the ear but exciting enough to move dancers to the floor. Soon, the floor was swimming with couples rocking away. The guitarist sounded very impressive now that he had tuned his instrument.

Fofo and the man turned to face the floor to see those dancing. Skirts flew in the air and shoes went clap-clap-clap on the cement floor. The dancers had really warmed up and so had the bandmen. The leader took a long solo on his trumpet. The crowd shouted, 'Blow, blow, blow' at this. This inspired him to pitch higher notes and,bending backwards, his eyes closed tight, he gave the crowd more solo. At the end of the solo, he laughed happily, obviously pleased with his performance. He took out a white handkerchief and mopped beads of sweat that were threatening to run down into his white shirt.

When the number ended, the dancers shouted for more. They remained on the floor waiting for it.

'Well, ladies and gentlemen, you have been listening and dancing to the famous Blue Bells Dance Band,' the bandleader announced into the microphone. Then turning to the boys, he snapped: 'A-one, a- two, a-one, two, three, fo...'

The band swung into another rock, this time a much faster one, at the end of which the dancers retired to their seats and did not ask for more.

'This band is good,' the man remarked.

'Yes, but I like the Happy Beats,' Fofo added.

'Yes, they are also good.'

'Grace has not come back,' Fofo said.

'She will come.'

'Grace can be funny sometimes.'

'Do you work together?' the man wanted to know.

'No, we went to school together.'

'Which school?'

Fofo's reply was drowned by the loudspeakers which announced the next number as a 'High Life.' It was a popular number and everybody started moving on to the floor.

'Shall we dance?' the man requested.

'Hmm?'

'I said let's go and dance,' he repeated, and got up.

Fofo looked towards the floor, then back to the man before getting up. It was now getting dark and the multi-coloured naked bulbs dotted around the club came alive. Halfway through the dance, the man held Fofo closer. He could feel her warm, firm breasts against his chest. The fragrance of her perfume rose and overwhelmed him. He inhaled exaggeratedly.

'Are you tired?' Fofo asked.

'No, I was inhaling your perfume.'

Fofo laughed. Though the laugh was not a forced one, she had not made up her mind what to make of the man. He was good-looking all right, but why should that concern her? A lot of young men were handsome and she could not fall for all of them. He had said he liked her. But so would all other men who wanted something from a girl.

'Do you think Grace will come back?' she asked.

'Yes, she will,' the man said, not caring whether she came back or not. He was holding Fofo in his arms and he liked the feel of her body, and Grace could vanish as far as he was concerned.

The guitarist moved up to the microphone and joined the leader in a vocal duet. They sang in such good harmony that at the end of the number, they patted each other on the back. It did not look as if the guitarist was going to get the sack after all.

Neither Grace nor her boyfriend came back for the rest of the evening. Fofo drank some more beer and danced with the man the rest of the session.

'I want to go and find out what happened to Grace,' Fofo said when they left the club.

'So when do I see you again?' the man asked.

'Do you want to see me again?'

'Yes.'

'Why?' she asked.

'Because I like you,' the man said.

'That's the second time you've said that.'

'Yes, and I mean that,' the man assured her.

'Ha, ha!' well, let's go and find out what happened to Grace.'

Determination, they say, is only a wish to achieve a purpose. Determination in itself does not constitute war. In the Akan language, this age-old philosophy is more eloquently put. And on the familiar mammy lorries that ply the townships and cities, echoes of this may be seen written up.

In spite of Fofo's determination to discover fulfillment as a woman, when finally she returned home that night, her virginity was intact. She had come close to losing it, but she could not just give it to the first man she met on the day she had determined to be laid. Not even though she had been taken to teatime dance by that man and had sipped his beer and pushed her firm breast against his chest on a dance floor. It takes more than that to conquer a girl like her. Not even dear Lawrence had been given the privilege. He was a devil all right, but at least she knew him longer and better than this man who called himself Kweku Ampoma. May be he was not even called Kweku Ampoma. Men could be such rogues you have to be on your guard all the time and no silly slips.

There was no light in Grace's room. Perhaps they were in, sleeping in the darkness. People did not go to bed that early in Accra, but then you never knew when a boy and his girlfriend were in.

Fofo tried the handle, but the door was locked. She peeped through the keyhole and was assured that her friend was not in. The stray beam of light from the street light enabled her to just see the better part of the room.

'She has not come home,' she told Kweku Ampoma.

'Oh!'

'I think she has gone to Kofi's place, she added.

The man cleared his throat. Fofo's heart missed a beat, or she knew what the man was going to say. She was not far wrong.

'Err...well, in that case, why don't we go somewhere?' the man suggested.

'Oh?'

'Yes, we can go to my place and listen to music.'

Aha, that's it, thought Fofo, he would finally want to coax me into his house. May be he has not even got a radio box in his house. He is going to take me into his room and stretch me on his iron bed and bleed me to death, ha, all for lousy beer.

'Well, what do you say?' he persuaded.

'I would love to come, but it is late and I have to go home and prepare food for my father,' Fofo managed to say convincingly.

'We shan't be long,' he persuaded.

Aha, that's it. Of course it does not take long. But sorry, wrong number, thought Fofo.

'Well, I really must go home and cook. Maybe another time.'

'When shall I see you again?'

'Oh, we shall meet again, Accra is not such a big place,' Fofo said.

'It is bigger than you think.'

'You give me your telephone number and I will ring you,' she said.

The man fished for a paper. He found an envelope in his back pocket but no pen to write with.

'Do you have a pen?' he asked.

'No.'

'I don't have one either.'

'Doesn't matter tell me, I will remember.'

'Will you?'

'Oh yes, I've got a good head for numbers,' Fofo assured him, and hailed a taxi. She jumped into it fast, slammed the door and asked the driver to drive on. She waved at the man. The man waved back and tried to smile. But the smile was dry and hard, and disappeared quickly.

'Dammit!' the man said and walked towards home.

Chapter 7

When Fofo's taxi pulled up in front of her home, she could hear her father's voice. She could recognise anger in the voice and she knew she had to be cautious not to aggravate the situation. Ataa Kojo obviously would not have nice words in store for her. She had insisted on going out when he had asked her to cook. Now she wondered whether it was worth flouting her father's orders. Perhaps it would be wiser to stay out till a little later when Ataa Kojo had calmed down. Perhaps she ought to have gone with Kwaku Ampoma to his house – just to find out if he really had music in his room. But it was late now, too late to just stand there debating over what could not be reconstructed. She would have to go into the house and bear the brunt of her father's displeasure. She walked into the house.

'Eee… Fofoooo…poooo! The voice that greeted her was warm and hearty. And although the speaker was in semi-darkness, Fofo could not mistake her elder sister's voice.

'Eeei … Sister Karley- oooooo pote. Yeee … and when did you come?' Fofo asked.

'Not very long, I was told you had gone out,' Karley said.

'Yes, I went to …'

'Oh, shut up and let me say what I am saying!' Ataa Kojo shouted her down. What he had been saying was giving his elder daughter a piece of his mind. For the second time in her marriage, Karley had packed her things and left her husband at Kumasi. This time she was not going back and when the new-born baby was able to walk and speak, she would send him to his father.

'Ataa Kojo, you do not know what that man has been doing to me. When I found out about this Ashanti woman, I asked him about it like any sane woman would.' Karley tried to tell her story, her sad story, to win her father to her side. But the old man stuck to his own ideas about husbands' waywardness.

'Listen, Karley, I do not know why you are telling me all that and I do not know why you women always go on about man's little pleasures in life. What you should know is that man is man and he is not bound to preserve his manhood to one woman alone. When you were in Kumasi, did you not notice that some of the Ashanti men had two, three, four wives? And that all the wives lived in the same house in harmony?' Ataa Kojo asked .

'But, father, how can you …'

'Oh shut up and let me talk. Let me tell you that nothing prevents a normal man to sleep with other women besides his wife. In fact, any man who sticks to his wife alone must be weak somewhere. You yourself said that he started sleeping with the Ashanti woman about three months ago. That means your position was such that he had pity on you and did not want to bother you. You ought to be grateful to him. But then woman is never grateful. Now you have packed your things and come here with your two-month-old baby. What do you want me to do with you two? Do you realise that I cannot feed you at your age any more? I expect you, at your age, to be remitting me every month, if you want to know. Do you not know that Chico is still at school and that that foolish brother of yours in Takoradi has not sent any money for the past two months? He had better not come home for the Homowo this year. If he does, he would have to show his foolish face with the arrears, otherwise death to him.'

Fofo laughed.

'You are laughing at your father, you so- and-so. You are just as daft as Karley. If you girls do get folks' sons to keep you in their homes, you ought to shut your mouths and do as they bid.'

'Even running after other women?' Fofo asked.

'Nonsense, every normal male will go after other women. That's the way God created us. So Karley, I suggest that tomorrow morning, you get yourself together and go back to your husband in Kumasi. Do you understand that?'

'I for one will not go back to that man,' Karley said.

'Then you will have to get out of this house. This house belongs to your brothers and their wives,' Ataa Kojo said with finality. Karley started weeping.

'Don't cry, sister Karley, I'm sure everything is going to be all right,' Fofo consoled her. As if by common design, the baby on her sister's lap also woke up from his sleep and started crying.

'He must be hungry. Give him to me, I will give him some breast milk,' Fofo said.

'Some what?' her elder sister stopped whimpering and asked.

'Breast milk. I've got breasts too, you know,' Fofo informed her sister.

'Tsu!' Karley uttered and dipping her hand beneath her *kaba*, she dug out one heavy breast and stuck the nipple into the crying mouth of her baby.

The baby's lips closed onto the nipple and started sucking the milk greedily. Fofo studied the little baby for a while.

'Soon, I will have a baby too,' she said.

'What, are you pregnant?' Karley asked.

'No,' Fofo replied with a laugh.

'But all women do have babies some time or the other.'

'Huh, the way you have started, you will be having a baby sooner than you think and you will not even know who the father is,' Ataa Kojo said.

'Father, I don't like that!' Fofo protested.

'But it's true. Where did you go this afternoon?'

'I only went to see Grace.'

'Liar!'

'Oh, Ataa Kojo, you never trust anybody in this house,' Fofo said.

'Trust died a long time ago. How can I trust you children any more when Chico, at his age, knows what's between a woman's legs? Oh, curse the days I had you lot,' he said.

The revelation surprised Karley. She stared at her father for a long time, then turned to Fofo.

But Fofo got up and went into her room.

'Chico?' Karley asked Ataa Kojo.

The old man also got up and went into his room.

'Eh, Chico! What has this world come to now? Hmm ... Ataa Naa Nyumo eee!' Karley moaned.

Chapter 8

Chico did not know of his elder sister's arrival from Kumasi. He had gone out to play table tennis with Addo. This was to tune himself up for a major tournament with one of the schools in the city. Chico's school had lost to them last year and they had not taken the defeat lightly, especially as they had anticipated victory. So far this year, they had beaten all the schools they had played and Achimota was to be the next.

As far as Chico was concerned, it meant everything to him. He had created a sensation as the up and coming player with the dynamite smashes. His picture had appeared in the popular press and he had even been discussed on radio as a talent to be reckoned with.

When finally they ended the training session, he was tired and hungry. On his way back home, he bought some groundnuts at the Bukom Square.

'Chico, Chico!' a woman's voice called. He turned.

The voice belonged to Maami Adoley, the elderly kenkey seller whom, according to Fofo, their father used to flirt with.

'Good evening, Ma Adoley,' he greeted her.

'How are you?'

'Fine.'

'Eh Chico, I saw you in the Graphic the other day.'

'Me , in the Graphic?'

'Yes, your picture. Or was that not you? I thought it was you, was it not?' Ma Adoley asked. Chico smiled.

'Ah, you see, I knew it was you. You must have done something good at school, not so?'

'Yes,' Chico replied with a smile.

'You've done well. Keep it up.'

'I will try.'

'Don't try, just do it.'

'Yes, Ma,' Chico said and turned to go.

'Eh, I hear Karley is back from Kumasi,' the woman hinted.

'Who?'

'Karley, your sister. I hear she has returned form Kumasi.'

'Oh, I did not know that.'

'You have not been home then?'

'No, I went to a friend.'

'Hmm... then you would not know. Anyway I hear she has come. If you go home bid her welcome and say I will come to the house tomorrow,' Madam Adoley said.

'Yo-o,' Chico said and walked thoughtfully towards home.

The last time he saw Karley was last year, during the Homowo. She only returned to Accra once a year together with her husband. And each time, too, she stayed with the husband at the husband's family house near the lagoon. It was not yet time for the Homowo festival, so what had she come to do anyway? Not that Chico disliked his elder sister. He was always pleased to see her; and what was more, Karley was disposed to generosity towards him more than Fofo. What he was not happy about was that his elder sister's stay in the house meant that he would have to move into Allotey's room. He did not fancy this very much, for at one time he used to share that room with Allotey and he had not liked it one bit. Several times, Allotey had returned home in the middle of the night with a prostitute. He would wake Chico up and ask him to go out for a few minutes while he attended to the midnight female friend. Chico would spend about half an hour in the cold of the open before he would be allowed to return to sleep., He would return to the room and find it stinking of cheap cigarette smoke and sweat. He would lie awake for the rest of the night, knowing that sleep would only bring him nightmares of what his elder brother and the nameless prostitute had done in the room.

He could not move and share his father's room because Ataa Kojo too, at his age, would occasionally entertain a female at night. But tonight, it did not look as if anybody would slip a woman into the house. Karley had returned from Kumasi, and the chances were that the family would sit and talk for the better part of the night. The night had already begun and when Chico arrived home, Ataa Kojo, Karley and Fofo were eating together.

'Eh Chico, eh little brother Chico-o-o!' Karley serenaded.

'Yiee, sister Karley, it's been a long time since I saw you. When did you arrive?' Chico asked, and without waiting for a reply, he picked up a bucket nearby, turned it upside down and sat on it to join in the food.

'Go away, Chico, go and wash your dirty hands!' Fofo shouted at her brother.

'Oh. I'm hungry,' Chico protested.

'Oh get away! Who sent you?'

'Go and wash your hands!' his father bellowed.

Chicho sprang up, washed his hands and presently returned to table. He ate like a wolf.

'Oh Chico,' Karley said with a laugh. They watched him eat. Ataa Kojo got up to wash his hands. He drank some water and re-positioned his chair so that he could sit leaning against the wall. He always did that after his last meal of the day. It was a healthy thing to do – he had often said. Allows the food to sink properly, and make room for a shot of his usual *Akpeteshie* on roots – which was also good for the health.

'Chico, where have you been?' Karley asked.

'Went to play table tennis.'

'Oh yes, you were in the papers some time ago,' Karley said.

'Yes.'

'You did well.'

'Yes.'

'How is school?'

'Fine.'

'How are you doing with the girls?'

'What girls?'

'I hear you've already started ...'

'Lies, all lies,' Chico protested and stopped eating.

'Oh eat on,' Karley entreated.

'Listen, sister Karley, I know Fofo has been telling you things about me and I will tell you that they are all lies,' Chico said.

'You would say that, wouldn't you?' Fofo retorted.

'Nonsense!'

'Don't say that to Fofo, she is your elder sister,' Karley reminded him.

'But she is annoying me!'

'Well, eat up,' she said persuasively.

Chico ate up and cleared the things.

'Have you finished?' his father asked.

'Yes,' Chico replied.

'Well, go and bring my bottle from my room,' the old man instructed. He meant the bottle containing *Akpeteshie* on roots.

'Where is it?' Chico asked.

'Near my bed, stupid!' Ataa Kojo was impatient.

Chico emerged with the bottle. There were roots in the bottle all right, but the gin was almost down to the bottom. Ataa Kojo took the bottle and eyed the contents suspiciously.

'Someone has been drinking my gin behind my back!' he shouted with displeasure.

'Not me.' Chico denied.

'Not me.' Fofo also denied.

'So who did?' Ataa Kojo asked again.

'Well not me. I wouldn't drink stuff like that,' Fofo said.

'What the devil do you mean by that?' the old man demanded.

'Akpeteshie is not a good drink,' Fofo replied.

'Foolishness. It is better than the ones they import. This is good for the health,' Ataa Kojo insisted.

'Purely a matter of opinion,' Chico commented.

'Shut up!' the old man barked. All his children laughed.

Karley dipped her hand into her brassiere and fished out some coins.

'Chico, here, go and buy four shillings worth for Ataa Kojo.'

They talked into the night, and, inspired by the gin, Ataa Kojo did most of the talking. And when they finally retired to bed, Allotey had still not returned from town.

Chico moved his things into his elder brother's room and slept deep.

In the middle of the night, Allotey returned to discover Chico in his room.

'Hey, Chico , Chico, wake up!'

'What?'

'Wake up!'

'I'm sleeping.'

'You can't sleep here. Wake up and go to your own room,' Allotey ordered him.

Chico opened his eyes. His elder brother had brought a girl from town.

'I can't, Karley has come from Kumasi so Ataa Kojo says I should sleep here,' Chico explained.

'Well, then go outside for a few minutes.'

'I can't, I'm asleep,' Chico said and covered his head with his cloth.

Allotey's female companion became impatient.

'Tsu, you haven't got a place to sleep yet you brought me along. This is all a waste of time and money. I am going,' the woman said, and stormed away.

'This is all nonsense. I will leave this house and go and hire a room somewhere. My God, I will!' Allotey promised and lit a cigarette.

Chapter 9

The rain had stopped and the ban on drumming in the Ga traditional area had been lifted. The Homowo Festival was drawing near and the prospect of getting good fish for the festivities looked bright for the fishermen were beginning to net big catches at sea.

Karley did not return to her husband in Kumasi. She said that now that she was in Accra and the Homowo was close by, she might as well stay for it. Ataa Kojo did not object much to that; more particularly when he had had word from Karley's husband saying that he would explain the circumstances of Karley's departure. The message had come together with some money for his wife's upkeep; and as providence had willed it in the old man's favour, the money had fallen into the eager hands of Ataa Kojo.

'I think I will keep the money myself. After all, while you are here, I shall be looking after you and the cost of living, these days, is no child's play,' he told his daughter and turned a deaf ear to her subsequent violent protests.

Contrary to expectation, the oldman did not spend the money frivolously. He decided that he would use part of it to buy drinks for the festivities. Hitherto, he had almost entirely depended on his eldest son, Martey, for the few drinks he would bring from Takoradi. Martey had always managed to obtain rare brands of whisky and gin from the ships that docked at the Takoradi Harbour. And each time elders and relations called on Ataa Kojo to extend their Homowo felicitations, he would bring out a bottle and employ a great deal of lip to draw the visitors attention to the excellent brand of the drink and how much money he had spent to get it from beyond the sea. Things that came direct from European countries were the best one could be blessed with, in Ataa Kojo's view. What they produced was the best. Their way of thinking was also the best, thought Ataa Kojo. 'Kwame Nkrumah would make us believe the contrary, but he does not know a thing or two. He is a young man with a lot of heat in his head; but we who were born when Ghana was Gold Coast know a damn good drink by the look of it. And when it comes to real tradition and customs as laid down by the gods of the land, he will have to learn from us.'

Preparations for the festival were gathering momentum. The boat race by the fishermen had taken place. It had been an exciting affair which had drawn a large number of people. Several Europeans who had come to the country for their summer holidays had been there, taking still pictures and running their 8mm movie cameras; for the winning crew, it was a thing to boast about for a whole year. That particular night meant a lot of jubilation and lots of booze. The drumming of Kolomashie could be heard in the square miles away all night. The words of the songs that they sang to the drumming reflected the strength and tough muscles of the winning team. And that was why all the pretty girls with large breasts and big bottoms came to them; they had the best a man could offer a woman who had such good things to offer. The offspring of a member of the victorious team is always a winner.

Fofo and Karley were at the square to watch the drumming and dancing. The participants had white calico round their necks or heads to signify victory. Their supporters could also be identified by the same badge.

Elbowing his way through the crowd towards the two sisters was Lawrence. He had spotted Fofo from a distance. Lawrence had not seen her in a long while. The truth was that he had stopped hanging about the girl he had long fancied since the days when they were both working in the same firm. But Fofo had been difficult to persuade to do the things he wanted to do, and he had given up trying when he came across someone who was more accommodating.

'Hey, Lawrence, is that you?' Fofo shouted with excitement.

She had always been fond of Lawrence but had not decided whether to open up to him.

'Yes, it's me all right – body and soul.'

'Haven't seen you for a long time,' Fofo said.

'No.'

'Oh, that's bad. Why don't you ask me out?'

'No time.'

'Oh that's too bad. I thought you liked me.'

'I do, but sometimes it's…'

Fofo cut him short for she knew the cause of his indifference.

'Oh, I know, as for you boys…' They both laughed.

'I saw you at the seaside,' Lawrence said.

'Oh, is that so? Why didn't you call me?'

'You were far away, besides it was after the race, so I had to drive away quickly before I was caught up in the crowd.'

Fofo's eyes lit up with excitement.

'Drive away, does that mean you have a car?' she asked.

'No, it's only a scooter. I bought it two months ago.'

'So?'

'Yes, brand new. I've parked it on the main street.'

'Oh, let's go and see it!' Fofo requested.

'All right.'

And without saying anything to her elder sister, she followed Lawrence. The crowd was so thick, it was not easy to make their way through. Lawrence therefore grabbed Fofo's hand and held her close behind him so that she could inch her way into the gap her companion managed to create.

Finally, they got into the main street and heaved a sigh of relief.

'Where is it, Lawrence?'

'Over there.'

'Oh, its new!' Fofo exclaimed.

'Brand new,' the boy said and sparked it. He gave a few noisy revs and turned to Fofo.

'Shall I give you a ride?' he said.

'Oh, me?'

'Why not?'

'I'm afraid.'

'Nothing to be afraid of. You just sit behind me and hold me tight. Even my little sister rides behind me and she is not afraid,' the boy encouraged her.

'So?'

'Yes, come on, sit here.' He mounted Fofo on the passenger pillion.

'Now hold me very tight,' he advised.

'Like this?'

'No, put both hands round me and hold very tight like my sister does,' the boy encouraged her.

Fofo did as she was told. The boy pushed the scooter forward to release it from the resting position. They rode off. The girl held on fast to him and did not even realise how hard her firm breasts were pressing him.

'It's nice, ha, ha, ha!' giggled Fofo.

'I told you, even my sister does it,' the boy repeated.

'I like it, ha, ha, ha!'

'Yes, I know. I tell you what, let's go for a drink somewhere,' Lawrence said.

'A drink, let's go for a drink!' he shouted over the scooter's noise.

'All right, ha, ha, ha!' she agreed with a laugh.

were both hot and perspiring, longing for something
cold to drink. They started the second bottle before they
were aware that a short while ago their bodies had been
very close and that she had had her arms folded around
his waist and that he had felt her young breasts pressing
against his body.

'That was nice,' he said.

'The beer?'

'No, I mean the ride.'

'Yes, ha, ha!

'You have a warm body,' he said.

'How do you know?'

'Ah …Never mind. Drink up, I'm thirsty myself,' he
said and drank from his glass. When he set it down, Fofo
made an attempt to fill it.

'No, don't, I'm the driver. You pour it into yours.'

'No, I will get drunk.'

'Doesn't matter, I know your house,' Lawrence said.

But when they left the beer bar and mounted the
scooter, the boy drove towards his house.

'Where are we going?' Fofo asked.

'We are going to my house. I have to change my shirt.
Can't you feel how wet it is?'

'It doesn't matter, my pants are wet too,' the girl
informed him.

'Please don't take them off here.'

They both burst out laughing, as the driver turned the scooter into a house.

'Is this where you live?' the asked.

'Yes.'

'Your parents live here too?'

'No, I rent my own room here.' The boy said.

It was a bed-sitter. The bed was an iron bedstead and neatly made with coloured sheets. There were three armchairs and a centre table. Next to the bed was a wireless set.

'This is where I live,' he informed her.

'Nice.'

'Sit down,' he said.

The girl sat down and put her legs together. The boy smiled and sat next her.

'You were going to change your shirt,' she reminded him.

'Yes. Well, help me undo the buttons.'

The girl obliged.

They boy looked at her face steadily and took her head in his hands.

'You are pretty.'

'Your shirt is wet.'

'I love you, Fofo,' he said and dropped his hands to the girl's waist.

He squeezed it. Fofo gasped with fear.

'Don't hurt me, Lawrence,' she pleaded.

'I will be gentle.' The boy promised. He slowly raised the girl and led her to the bed.

'I am afraid, Lawrence.'

'I will be gentle,' the boy repeated, and switched off the light.

Fofo did not resist in the dark. Not because she wanted it, but because her mind was preoccupied with how painful-pleasant the experience would be. She had no objection to opening up her inner soul for Lawrence to enter. Accepting him would not amount to throwing herself away. To her, she would be letting her door open for a man who had long professed love to her, but whom she had not hitherto considered as a possible bedfellow. She had been fond of him as a woman would be of a man but had not equated this affection in terms of sex. She had considered sex as an extension of love, complete and sealed.

Womanhood, they say, comes to some women easily and as naturally as it was meant to be; but to others, nature is a bit harsh and unpropitious. Fofo had felt that there was no particular hurry for a thing which would happen to her anyway, some day. She had preserved her virginity till now, at a time when she had not been thinking about it. She had just been thrown into a situation to which she did not object.

To her, it was better that way than going after fulfillment like a dog chasing a bone. Come to think of it, a dog going after bone is also natural, but then human beings are not dogs.

They both lay silently in the dark. It was painful for her, but now it was all over and she no longer remembered how painful it had been. Perhaps it was not even painful at all. She had gasped and cried a little, but now she could breathe freely and the tears had now dried. She felt rather tired and wet.

'Shall I put on the light?' the boy asked, breaking the silence.

'No, please, no.'

'You shy?' he asked.

Fofo did not reply.

The boy got down from the bed.

'Don't put on the light!' Fofo said, almost screaming.

'I am not going to put on the light. I only want to open the window to let in fresh air, I'm sweating,' he said.

'Well, after a thing like that, you would sweat, wouldn't you?' she teased.

The boy laughed and opened the windows.

The August moon was full and the stars twinkled as if they were happy for Fofo. A gust of sea breeze blew gently through the window curtains and into the room. The feel of the night air on Fofo's naked body was most welcome to her. She had also been sweating.

The boy returned to the bed and lay close to her. His hands moved playfully over her body.

'Are you tired?' he asked.

'Are you not?' the girl asked in reply.

'No.'

'Well, I am,' she said.

The boy smiled and kissed her lightly on the lips. The girl put her arms round the boy and held him close to her breasts. She held him for a long time and when finally her embrace relaxed, she fell asleep.

Fofo did not know how long she had been sleeping, but when she woke up, she could hear the local broadcasting stations playing the national anthem to close the day's transmission. The room was still dark but for the glow of the panel light from Lawrence's wireless set.

He was not on the bed and there was no indication of his presence in the room either.

'Larry,' she whispered.

There was no reply.

She got out of bed and switched on the light. Her pants were lying at the foot of the bed. The dress which the boy had neatly hung on the chair was not creased.

She stood in the middle of the room, not knowing what to do. Her eyes caught her naked image in the mirror of the boy's dressing mirror. Slowly she turned and faced it. What she saw was not what she been seeing whenever she looked at herself after a bath. What she saw was the body of the new Fofo, the Fofo who had discovered womanhood, and the experience of accepting a man into her soul. A deep sense of satisfaction overwhelmed her. She smiled.

She took her pants and slipped them on. She dressed and examined her hair. It had not been badly ruffled, as she had expected. She had neatly plaited it in traditional fashion and all she needed was to brush down the stray strands of her hair back into place and no one would notice anything.

She sat down and wondered where Lawrence had gone. The wireless set was making a hissing noise. The station had close down and the set was just wasting electricity. She got up and tried to switch if off.

The door opened and Lawrence came in.

'You are awake,' he said.

'Yes.'

'I thought I would have a bath. Do you want a bath?'

'No, I will do that when I get home. It must be late, G.B.C. has just closed down.' Fofo said.

'Let me try another station.' Lawrence said and began to tune the radio, he got the Voice of America and the programme was Music U.S.A. and the man was playing jazz. Ella Fitzgerald was doing a number with the Count Basie orchestra.

'I like jazz music. Do you know jazz originated from Africa?' he asked.

'Who said so?'

'Oh yes, the negroes took it there. You know they used to sing them on the cotton plantations as work songs, then they sang them in church as gospels,' the boy informed her.

'I want to go home,' the girl said.

'Okay, I will get dressed and take you.'

'I can't ride behind the scooter. I feel tired,' she said.

Lawrence laughed and promised to take her home by taxi.

'No, I would rather go home alone.'

'Now don't be silly, Fofo, it's late. Then there was the blues. You know, they used to wail to the guitar. They were sad people, you know.'

'Who?' the girl asked.

'The negroes, you know, the slaves who were taken to America to work on the cotton plantations. They sang the "blues" right from their souls.'

'I am going home,' the girl said.

'All right, let's go.'

When Fofo got up, the boy caught her in his arms and kissed her deep on the lips.

'It's late,' she said.

'Let's go then.'

They went out.

The street was almost deserted and the first taxi they hailed did not stop.

'Bastard!' Lawrence hurled the insult after it.

They walked on in silence. Occasionally, they would pass other couples now returning from the cinema.

'They say there is a new film at the Royal,' Lawrence said to break the silence.

'I don't like going to the cinema these days.'

'Oh, why not? I was going to take you to see it. I hear it's good,' he said.

Fofo did not say anything to that. She seemed to be seriously thinking about something. The truth was that she was not thinking about anything. She had just thought it best to be silent. And what would one want to talk about with a man who had just taken one's virginity anyway? Words had not been necessary in the first place. Drive her to his house and sleep with her, just like that, and without resisting? What kind of give-away was that?

'Are you angry?' the boy asked.

'About what?'

'Well, I thought you were angry.'

'I am,' Fofo said. 'You should know; forcing me like that.'

'Oh, I am terribly sorry, but I did not mean to force you,' the boy said apologetically, though he knew that what he had done with her amounted to nothing like rape. But then, anything to make her happy. Wasn't that just like a woman? Always being wronged by men even if they condoned it. Dammit, what was she complaining about anyway? Had he not longed for a chance like this for years? And when it came at a time he least expected it, must he let it go?

'Well, I am sorry, girl, but you are a pretty girl and I have always loved you, and have always wanted to hold your firm breasts and enter your soul with my spirit. Now I see it was worth waiting for,' he said and smiled.

'You are laughing,' Fofo said.

'No, I am only glad that I have known the sweetest girl in the whole of Accra,' the boy said.

'Anything to flatter me just because you have got what you want.'

'That's unfair.'

'Is it?'

'Yes, I love you, Fofo .' the boy said.

Fofo did not say anything till they reached Bukom. She stopped.

'What's the matter?'

'I think you'd better leave me just here. I will be all right.' She said.

The boy insisted on leading her to the house but Fofo refused.

'Somebody will see us and the whole neighbourhood will start singing my name.'

'But it is late.'

'It's all right. It is only a few yards to my house and there are people still in the square.'

'All right, then. When do I see you again?' Lawrence wanted to know.

'You will not see me in that house again. Good night,' she said and walked away.

'Good night,' the boy said and watched Fofo disappear in the night. He then jumped high and yelped with excitement.

'Yiee ho!'

The exhilaration of having broken new ground overwhelmed him. He swung into whistling a gay tune as he hurried to his house.

Everybody was asleep in Fofo's house. She went straight to the bathroom to urinate. Her elder sister was fast asleep but had remembered not to lock the door. However, she woke up when Fofo opened it.

'Who is that?' Karley asked.

'It's me,' Fofo replied.

'Where have you been?' Karley wanted to know.

Fofo did not reply. She took off her sandals and removed her earrings. She drank some water from an enamel cup beside the bed, before lying down.

She slept like a baby.

Chapter 10

The late train from Kumasi pulled in at the Accra station. Its arrival was heralded with boundless enthusiasm from the crowd who had come to meet their relations. Some of them tried to get on it while the train was still in motion and the station guards had a job keeping them away.

The locomotive driver, clad in a dark blue suit with brass buttons and a cap, his tired face made darker by the long exposure to soot and smoke from the engine, congratulated himself on having driven the passengers safely to Accra. His ego was further boosted by the anxious crowd at the station. He smiled and blasted the train's whistle unnecessarily long in a manner George Stephenson would not have approved.

Karley's husband, Mr Odoi, was one of the first passengers to alight from the train. He did not have much luggage and this made it possible for him to elbow himself through the crowd. He did not stand on the pavement, craning his neck to scan faces in the crowd because he was not expecting anybody to meet him. He had not told anybody when he would arrive for the Homowo. He did not have to tell anybody. Accra was not a strange town to him and he could always make his way to his house and find a welcome.

Although the last time he saw the city was just five months ago when he came down on a two-week-leave, he was not expecting it to look like Tolayo in five months in spite of serious development in the municipality. The changes he saw were just what he expected. Old dilapidated buildings pulled down here and there and new structures taking their places. Taxi drivers had not changed; they still blew their horns as if everybody else was stone deaf. Women still hawked petty items on the pavements along the streets. Unsightly beggars, holding their calabashes at arm's length, still asked passers-by for *salaka*. The Makola markets were still busy and the market mammies were still fat. The City Council was still fighting the problem of keeping the municipality clean. They still blamed this on folks refusal to pay their basic rates. But, well, what could one do about it? Karley's husband, for example, had never paid basic rate in his life. He had always said that he did not live in the city, so why should he pay? And he never paid in Kumasi either; because he had always told the collectors over there that he paid his rates in Accra. And with so many people like him refusing to pay their basic rates to help keep the city clean, the City Council was bound to have problems.

After all, you cannot have a city in Africa spotlessly clean. Where would the flies go then? And flies too are

God's creation, and all living things must eat. The trees eat, the birds eat, snails eat and worms also eat. Even the sea eats, and that's how God made it. Otherwise, why was it that each year, the chief fetish priest carried food to it during Homowo? And why do rivers feed it by carrying dead bodies into it?

These were some of the man's ruminations as the taxi drove him towards Bukom. He knew his people would be pleased to see him and he looked forward to it. He also knew that Ataa Kojo, his father-in-law, would be pleased to see him. But he was not looking forward to that. For one thing, Ataa Kojo would be expecting a bottle of gin from him and he had not bought one nor had any intention of doing so. Times had been hard since the government started taking part of his salary as income tax, and for another thing, he knew that his wife, Karley, had made a long complaint about the other woman to her father and he would have to prepare himself for an unpleasant confrontation with his father-in-law.

The wicked smile which played about his lips was not due to the thought of the confrontation, but to reminiscences of his affair with the other woman. And in spite of the repeated nagging he had suffered from his wife following his affair, he felt that the memory was worth more than a smile. The experience was worth reliving.

He had been posted to Kumasi as a young agriculture officer to help augment the staff engaged in rehabilitating the cocoa industry in the Ashanti Region. His job was to go into the field, inspecting cocoa farms and advising the farmers on the need to rehabilitate their crops. This had not been easy, considering the rate of illiteracy among cocoa farmers at the time and their suspicion of government officials who sit in their offices and claim to know more about farming than they themselves who live by the land. But the job had its rewards. Winning the confidence of farmers could bring its own peculiar rewards.

On one of his visits, Mr Odoi called on an old farmer, Kwesi Amponsah, with whom he had a form of friendship, perhaps on account of the good palm wine which was always available in the old man's village and to which he was always welcome.

'Oh officer, you are welcome. Please, here is a chair,' Amponsah's wife said to the man.

'Thank you, is your husband home or gone to the farm?'

'He has gone to Kumasi so see about some money. He did not say when he would be back.'

'I see. But he will return today?'

'Oh yes,' the farmer's wife agreed.

'I see.'

The woman then called her daughter to bring the officer some water to drink as custom demanded. Akosua Asantewa, a healthy nineteen-year-old girl, brought the water in a clean calabash. She did a slight curtsy with the presentation as was the custom with well-mannered rural females. The officer accepted it with a smile and sipped the water. Although the water had come from the pot and was cool, he was not particularly thirsty for water. As he returned the calabash to Akosua, his eyes caught a pair of breasts, full and firm, virtually protesting against the *kaba* the girl was wearing and looming out like a pair of boxer's gloves, held up nose-high for protection against an opponent. He smiled. Akosua smiled back shyly.

'Akosua, I think there is a pot of palm wine under the orange tree over there, bring it for the officer, she added, 'I am sure it is good, my husband always keeps the best palm wine under that orange tree.'

She was right. The stuff was fresh and tasty, a far cry from anything he would get to drink in Kumasi itself.

'Akosua, when on earth are you going to wash these clothes in the river?' the mother asked.

'In a minute, mother, I want to feed the hen who hatched yesterday. I think she deserves it. Nine chicks at a go is something,' Akosua replied with a giggle.

'All right, hurry up,' the mother said.

Akosua finished feeding the hen, packed the dirty clothing into a bucket and left for the river side. Mr Odoi watched her as she left and really liked what he saw.

'Do you get much fish in the river these days?' he asked the farmer's wife.

'Oh yes, when my husband gets the time to fish, he usually brings home enough. However, he has been hanging his net for quite some weeks and I have to go to the market to buy dry salmon,' she complained.

'I like fishing,' the officer intimated.

'Do you know how to fish?' she asked with surprise.

'Oh yes. I used to fish in the lagoon back home when I was a kid. We used to spend Sundays fishing and would return home with our catch and stinking like the lagoon itself,' he said.

This brought laughter from the woman.

'Then perhaps you want to try it in the river?' she questioned.

'Well, yes.'

'The net is over there.'

'Good. But if you do not see me again, then the river has taken me away and you may probably find my body in the sea in Accra. Ha, ha that would be the cheapest means of transport for dead bodies.'

'Oh officer, you are very funny.'

'I'm sure it is the palm wine. It is so good I can't help making silly jokes about serious things. Anyway, I think I will try fishing in the river. Where is the fishing net?'

He got up, took the fishing net and left for the riverside, taking the same footpath Akosua had taken.

What he saw at the riverside would have inspired any artist's imagination. With the river rolling downstream in the background, and flanked on either side by tropical greenery, stood the solitary figure of the farmer's daughter naked from the waist up and gazing into the river. She had finished the washing and the clean clothes lay spread on the foliage drying. Suddenly, she took off the cloth round her waist, revealing her real womanhood. It was total and complete. Full breasts, firm and defiant, and ready for plucking. She gingered her way into the river and timidly splashed into its waters.

Mr Odoi stood there watching, gasping and gaping for a while, but the girl did not notice him. Then he decided that it was time for him to start fishing. He walked to the bank of the river and called out to the girl. She looked up.

'Hey, what are you doing here?' she asked with a smile.

'Come to fish,' he replied.

'The fish is further downstream.'

'I like it here.'

'You won't get fish here.'

'I will try.'

'All right, as you please,' she said.

Mr Odoi took off his shoes.

'Is it cold down there?' he asked.

'Yes.'

'Good,' he replied and took off his shirt.

'Can you fish?'

'Yes,' he said and took off his trousers.

The girl laughed.

'What's the matter?'

'There's no hair on your chest.'

'It doesn't matter, there's plenty on my head and other places …'

He took the net and waded into the water. When he had got near enough, he threw the net over the girl and started drawing her towards him like captured fish. Her white teeth shone like pearls as she giggled and allowed herself to be pulled. When finally he took her body in his arms, it was full and warm in spite of the cold waters of the river.

The passing current of the river's cold waters beat on their bodies as they stood in one tight unity. The farmer's daughter started giggling at the tickling sensation. When she stopped, her eyes closed in maze and for a moment, they both lost their balance and fell off their feet. If the river had insisted, the current would have carried them away. Some rivers object to their waters being desecrated. But obviously, this river was a propitious deity and it was said that she was a goddess who could bless barren women with children if they prayed and made the necessary sacrifice to her.

Mr Odoi regained his balance quickly, grabbed Akosua's hand firmly and pulled her.

'Let's get out of the river,' he said.

'But I don't have anything on,' the girl complained.

'It doesn't matter now. I don't have anything on either,' he said and led her to the bank.

The sun was high and its rays slitted through the trees casting patterns of shadows below.

'Let's lie here,' he said.

'I'm wet,' she protested.

'Me too,'

'I want to dry myself first.'

'Go ahead.'

He watched her mop up with a towel. Her hands moved deftly round her body, efficiently passing the towel in places where water could be lodged. It was methodical and very feminine.

'Don't look at me,' she protested.

'I will close my eyes.'

He did not close his eyes.

'You haven't closed your eyes,' she reminded, and threw the towel at him.

'You can dry yourself too.'

'There is no need now, I am already dry.'

'You are a bad man.'

'It doesn't matter. Bring your cloth and spread it here,' he ordered.

The girl giggled and obeyed.

'What are you going to do?'

'We are going to lie down.'

The officer pulled her gently to the ground.

'You are a bad man.'

'You are a bad girl.'

He took her head in his hands and planted a noisy kiss on her lips.

'Why did you do that?' Akosua asked.

'It means you are beautiful,' he explained.

'Then do it again,' she pleaded.

The man did it again. This time less noisily and it lasted longer. When he stopped, her eyes were closed.

'Don't stop,' she whispered.

The man pulled her closer and went in.

The sun had gone down towards the West when Mr Odoi opened his eyes. He could see crimson ray of the setting sun reflecting on the running waters of the river. The world was much quieter, and the green leaves of the trees much still. The gentle breeze that blew on their naked bodies had the smell of natural greenery that one did not experience in the synthetic world of city life.

Akosua was still fast asleep.

'Hey, hey!' he called.

She did not hear.

'Akosua, hey, Akosua!' he called again, this time shaking her gently.

'Mmmmmm ...?'

'Wake up!'

'What?'

'I said wake up!'

She opened her eyes. When she saw the man, she smiled and said, 'You are a bad man.'

'You are a sweet woman.'

'You are strong.'

'I have no hairs on my chest.'

'Doesn't matter,' she said with a laugh, got up, pulled a cloth around herself and started picking up the now dry washing from the foliage.

The man got up and dressed.

The washing neatly folded and packed in the bucket, Akosua went back into the river.

'Are you not going to the village?' he asked.

'I must have a bath first.'

'I thought you had one before.'

'You did not let me. Go home, my father must have returned by now.'

'I will wait for you.'

'No, no, no! You go without me. I will follow later.'

'All right. Now where is the net?'

'What net?'

He had foolishly forgotten about the fishing net, and in the midst of his animal exuberance, had let the net go downstream.

'Now what shall I say?' he asked.

He had not much to say some months later, when a delegation from the village had confronted him with Akosua's pregnancy. He had accepted responsibility, with shame, and Akosua had come to live in Kumasi with an aunt so that he could take full responsibility for her till her delivery.

The smile disappeared from Mr Odoi's face as the taxi turned into the lane leading to his house in Bukom. The memory of that river experience had been worth reliving, but it was definitely not the kind of story one tells one's father-in-law.

That evening, after a bath and a good meal, he put on his best shirt and polished his shoes.

'Are you going to see your father-in-law?' his mother asked.

'Yes.'

'What are you taking with you?'

'Nothing.'

'Don't be a disgrace! Don't you know that when you're going to see your wife's father, you must take some drink with you?'

'Well, I have not got any drink to take with me,' he said.

'Oh, you are such a miscreant, you would go and disgrace our family in public and not know what the devil you are doing. You will never grow up. Well, there is such a thing as custom, you know,' the mother scolded.

'Custom be hanged! Drinks are expensive these days!'

'Don't stand there talking like a fool. Go into my room, there is a bottle of whisky in the cane basket. I bought it when I went to Lome last time. Take it.'

'Oh, thank you, mother.'

'And you may pay the cost of it if you like,' she added.

He did not answer that, which meant that he had no intention of paying for the whisky. If it was a gift from his mother, then it was a gift. And you do not pay for a gift. That would amount to an insult. And he did not want to insult his mother.

Without another word to his mother, he dashed out, the bottle of whisky neatly wrapped in an old newspaper, and walked towards Ataa Kojo's house.

Martey, Ataa Kojo's eldest son, had arrived from Takoradi with his wife some hours earlier. They were sitting in the compound of the house chatting. They had just heard Karley's story of her husband's affair with an Ashanti woman, and they had told her to have patience since all men were created polygamous. Martey had been landed in this direction for he too had been in a similar predicament with a Fanti woman in Takoradi. The only difference was that his wife, also of Bukom stock, had insisted on the girl having an abortion. It had been a very expensive insistence. The girl had nearly died but for the industry of the government hospital where the girl had been rushed after the quack had messed her inside. The police had had wind of it and Martey had had to spend good money to prevent prosecution.

For Ataa Kojo's part, it was all fine, as long as he did not have to pay anything. And finer still, to him, was when Homowo came and his in-laws brought him drinks.

One could, therefore, see the gleam in his eyes when Mr Odoi, Karley's erring husband, appeared with something under his arm. And by nature, Ataa Kojo would not lift a finger against anybody who was presenting him with a bottle of something. And if Mr Odoi knew this of his wife's father, he would have had no cause to worry about a confrontation.

'Ah, here you are. I was just thinking about you,' Ataa Kojo said when he saw Mr Odoi.

'People walk with their names, as they say,' added Martey.

'Please, find yourself a chair,' Ataa Kojo said, pointing at the empty chair next to Karley.

He shook hands; first, with Ataa Kojo, then the others. As soon as he sat down, Karley got up.

'And where are you going to, Karley?' Ataa Kojo asked.

'I've got work to do.'

'Oh, sit down there, what do you mean?' the old man shouted.

Karley sat down.

'Now you may bring your husband some water to drink first,' he added.

Karley got up again. There was general laughter.

'Ha, women who love their husbands usually want to pretend they don't.'

'Don't mind her, Mr Odoi, she is just a child. Her mother was like that, always groaning about little things,' Ataa Kojo said, putting his son-in-law at ease.

But it did more than that to Mr Odoi. It gave him reassurance that his father-in-law was on his side.

He drank the water his wife brought and poured some to the ground. He explained why he had not come earlier – due to pressure of work at the office, his boss having gone on leave and he being the next in command had had to act, and so on. Karley had decided to come early because she wanted to see the boat race.

'Liar!' Karley interrupted.

Anyway he was glad all was fine and he brought a bottle of whisky to the old man to pour libation to the gods.

The whisky was duly accepted with thanks. Then followed a period of polite conversation during which no-one brought up the question of Mr Odoi's affair with the 'Ashanti Woman.'

Chapter 11

The Bukoni family celebrated the Homowo festival in the desired fashion. They sent the traditional food, Kpokpoi, to friends and relations and received some in return. As the head of the household, Ataa Kojo had performed the necessary customary rites. He had poured libation to the gods asking for, among other things, long life and peaceful matrimony for all the children.

Each year, heads of families repeat this prayer to the gods of the land: that they had inherited from their forefathers who had emerged from the sea thousands of years before; the land they cultivated and tilled; the land they had fought bloody battles to keep; the land which now seated their houses and provided resting place for the remains of their dead departed, and one day would also provide a resting place for Ataa Kojo.

But that day was not near yet. He still had more years to live and had no intention of dying before he had achieved his one ambition to build a flush toilet in the house. He had been fascinated by it since he first saw one and used it. That was years ago, when he first went into a whiteman's bungalow.

They had gone there in a group of four workers to carry out some repair work in the bungalow. He had seen this white bowl and tank with a chain hanging from it. He had asked what it was and had been told it was the whiteman's toilet.

'What? He does it into this fine white bowl?' he asked.

'That's right.'

'Hmm... whiteman really is a whiteman!' he remarked, and he had found an opportune time to slip into the place and use it. He had pulled the chain and water rushed into the white bowl and washed the damn thing into the bowels of the earth.

'Ah, whiteman really is a whiteman.'

Ataa Kojo had never forgotten it and had vowed there and then to have one in his home one day. And even at his age, when he no longer earned a salary but a meager pension, he still thought about it.

It was with this in mind that he summoned, at dawn, all his children for a meeting. The Homowo festivities had almost come to an end, and everybody would start getting to his station and back to work.

'I must say, if Ataa Kojo wakes everybody up at dawn for a meeting, then he must have something very important to tell,' Karley remarked.

'Well, I should damn well hope so. Spoiling my sleep like that,' Martey, the eldest, said with a yawn, then added, 'If I know my old man, I would say that he is going to remind everybody how important it is to send him money at the end of each month.'

There was general laughter at this.

Ataa Kojo emerged from his room and asked the children what the laughter was about.

'Oh, Martey said something funny. Nothing to do with you,' Karley volunteered a lie.

'Oh, I see,' the old man said and pulled a chair and sat down. He cleared his throat and spoke.

'Well, what I am going to talk about may sound foolish, but I think it is important; and I have better brains than all of you put together.'

'Ataa Kojo, please, it's too early for scolding,' Karley reminded.

'I'm not scolding. I'm telling you something you may not fully appreciate.'

'All right, let's hear you.'

'Good. Well, children, you all know that civilisation has come. Kwame Nkrumah said that now we are independent and therefore we are like Europeans, we should have the good things that Europeans have,' the old man began.

'Oh, did he say that?'Allotey interrupted. The old man eyed him sternly without a word.

'I'm sorry, I won't interrupt again.'

'You'd better not! Well, Nkrumah knows best, and that is why he is building a new harbour at Tema. And that is why he is building a big power house at Akosombo. The Europeans have all these things in their country but they did not build them here. All they did was steal our money and sleep with our women. But all that is past. Kwame has stopped everything and has asked us all to live like proper men, in total control of things that make a man civilised. Well, in this house, there is one thing we can do to make folks in Bukom realise that I, Ataa Kojo, and my children are forward-looking. We are going to do what will make folks envy us. We are going to build a toilet with a water closet!'

He waited for some reaction from the children. He got it. There was a silence which was nothing more than stifled laughter. They looked at each other's faces. Eventually, Allotey giggled.

'Yes, like I said, it may sound foolish but important. We are going to build the whiteman's toilet in this house and the neighbours are going to come here and beg us to use it. What I want from all of you is to contribute some money, every month, towards this project. Now I want your views on it,' he concluded.

Allotey cleared his throat and informed the meeting that he should be counted out for he was leaving the house.

'And where do you think you are going?'

'I've got myself a room in town.'

'It doesn't matter, you will still have to contribute. This is your home, this house belongs to you all.'

'This house belongs to you. It was left to you by your father. It only becomes ours when you die. Till then, everything you want to do with it or in it is your affair. Me, I'm leaving it,' Allotey said.

'Allotey, that's not the proper way to talk. If you don't want to contribute, say so. But don't talk like somebody who was not brought up properly.' Karley scolded.

Allotey opened his mouth to retort but Martey intervened.

'Why don't you shut up! You talk like a fisherman's son. Sending you to school has been a complete waste of money.'

'I'm glad you realise that, Martey,' the old man said.

'Well, Ataa Kojo, if you want to build yourself a whiteman's toilet, all well and good. But personally, I don't think it is necessary. Anyway, you may have your love for the whiteman's toilet. I will send you your usual money and if you want to use it in building a new toilet, than I cannot stop you. I still have to pay Chico's school fees.' Martey said.

'What about you, Karley?'

'I think it is a good idea. I personally like flush toilets. We have one at the government quarters where we live in Kumasi. It is more comfortable to use and the place does not stink and there are no flies, I think I like the idea and I will send you money every month.'

'That's my daughter! What about you, Fofo?'

'Well, all right.'

'All right what?'

'I mean I will help.'

'Fine.'

***

With the final festivities of the Homowo over, Martey returned to Takoradi. Karley spent another week in Accra during which the conflict between she and her husband was resolved. Her husband had had to pacify her and had been made to promise that he would not have a second child with the Ashanti woman.

When it was time to return to Kumasi, Karley and her husband were on the best of marital terms. For Ataa Kojo's part, he had always stood for harmony between man and wife. Man was born to err a little every now and then. But then, that was how God created him. One woman could not fulfill all the desires of a man and that was why God made more women than men. If a woman appreciated this fact and made less trouble in the house for her man, there would be harmony all the time. His own wife had appreciated this and that was why she had had a good married life, bless her memory, before she died. A good woman she had been. She had given him five children who had grown up and were now helping him to build a new toilet.

As for Allotey, he was just a fool born into the family to create variety. He had kept his word and left the house as he had promised. But never mind, he would come back one day. They always did.

The end of the Homowo festival also marked the beginning of the new school year. Having been made the assistant head prefect of the school, Chico had to live on the school premises. This was one of the conditions attached to the position. He had always been a day student for his father could not afford to pay the boarding fee. Life had not been easy for him, but turning down such an honour would break his heart. He had therefore discussed his problem with the headmaster.

'Your son is a good boy, Mr Bukoni, and we will do all we can to help. But as you see, this school did not get the full government subvention to enable us grant such help. All the same, since we have such great trust in your boy, we will grant him free boarding and lodging. All you have to do is pay his the usual fees for books, clothing and so on,' the headmaster said.

'Thank you, master. My boy is a good boy and I am happy you have made him a prefect.'

'An assistant to the prefect, ' he corrected.

'Yes.'

And so Chico moved to the school compound. It had not been easy either. The money Martey sent from Takoradi to Ataa Kojo, meant for Chico's fees went into the old man's project. He used it as a deposit for the toilet seat.

Chico complained to Maami Adoley, the kenkey seller, who had grown fonder of Chico since his appearance in the newspaper.

'Your father is a fool. He has never had any brains in his head. All his life, his picture has never appeared in the newspaper. And instead of thinking more about you who have elated him, he goes about spending his money on stupid projects like that,' Maami Adoley said and gave Chico money to buy Clark sandals and some clothing.

'Don't mind Ataa Kojo, let him build his toilet. I will help you any time you are in need,' she promised.

Chico was grateful. He would only have to come for that help for one year since he was in his final year. Then he would take a job at the government department and buy her a present.

As for Ataa Kojo, let him go ahead with his project.

Indeed, the old man was going ahead. First, he hired people to dig the septic tank. When this was almost completed, he had a visit from an official of the City Council.

'What's going on here?' he asked the diggers.

They told him what the digging was meant for.

'Whose home is this?'

'Ataa Kojo.'

'Call him.'

Ataa Kojo came.

'I'm from the City Council.'

'You are welcome.'

'I hear you are undertaking construction works here.'

'Yes, I'm building a toilet.'

'Where is your permit?'

'What permit?'

'Don't you have a permit...?'

'What kind of permit? I'm not building on government property. This is my own house and I do not need any permit to build in my own house.'

'Well, the government does not allow it.'

'Who said that?'

'The law?'

'You are the law?'

'No.'

'Well, then who is it?'

'The City Council.'

'The City Council cannot be the law. You tell me somebody who says he is the law. The City Council is not a human being. I cannot talk to him.'

'Well, if you erect any structure, the city council will have to pull it down as unauthorised.'

'Foolishness, this is foolishness!'

'Are you insulting me?'

'Yes, and if you do not get out of here, you will see what you won't like.'

'Like what?'

'You wait and see,' Ataa Kojo said, grabbed one of the pickaxes and made for the man.

The man did not wait to see what Ataa Kojo was going to do with the weapon. He took to his heels and quickly disappeared in the alleys.

Ataa Kojo knew that that was not going to be the last of the official. He knew that soon, the big man at the city council himself would come with him. But then, they would be welcome. In fact, they would be more than welcome, for Bukom was where anything could happen to officials who wanted to poke their noses into other people's affairs. It had never been difficult handling people like that. Bukom had always been a phenomenon whose force Kwame Nkrumah himself had always appreciated. You do not walk into Bukom and tell them what to do. Folks with good heads on their shoulders go there to ask them to help do what they want to do. You have to be with them. You have to join them first, identify yourself with them. The politicians had always recognised this. And that was why, each time they went to give political speeches there, they hired kolomashie drummers and wore ordinary T-shirts. And having asked and received their votes to obtain a seat in parliament or the city council, no politician would want to go back to Bukom and want to lord it over them. They had responded to the 'Freedom' slogan, and freedom was freedom and no fooling.

Freedom to live like human beings and build new toilets if they so wished. And who was that silly little fly of an official who thought he could just come and throw his weight about? Where the devil was he when Kwame said folks should improve their living standards and that better living standards meant mature nation-hood? Did he not know why they built a new palace for the Ga Mantse?

Ataa Kojo's faith in the 'new order' was absolute. He was not, however, interested in the rationale or maxim behind it. He had welcomed it voluntarily as one would welcome the dawn of day. It had to come, he had heard it told, and like the dawn, one had to welcome it as the beginning of a new day. Unless of course, one had reasons for not wanting to see the new day. Ideology, as shouted by the politicians, meant nothing to him. If he liked you, he liked you and fine talk or brass band music would not change it. He was not limp in the mind. His mind was his own and his mind was a good mind, a strong mind. When he saw a thing, he looked at it. And when he did not like what he saw, he did not like it. And when he liked it, not even the law had a right to tell him otherwise.

'He will come back tomorrow,' commented the mason working on the septic tank.

'I know, but I'll be waiting for him,' Ataa Kojo said.

'Should I go on with the work?'

'I'm paying you, am I not?' Ataa Kojo asked.

'You are.'

'Good, then do what I pay you to do and leave that son of a lizard to me.'

For a whole week, that son of a lizard did not show his face. When he did finally, he was accompanied by the assistant to the city town engineer. Ataa Kojo was calm. He listened, attentively, as the engineer propounded and explained, at length, tenets of the law on unauthorised constructions within the confines of the municipality.

'Mister, what is your name?' Ataa Kojo wanted to know.

'Lamptey.'

'Lamptey, then you must come from this neighbourhood.'

'Well...'

'It doesn't matter if you don't want to own up. All Lampteys, all good genuine Lampteys, come from this neighbourhood. But being a big man, you don't live here any more. You probably live in a government bungalow – where do you live?'

'Me?'

'Yes, you.'

'Well, I live in a government bungalow.'

'I thought you did. And if it had not been for Kwame Nkrumah, you would still be living in this neighbourhood and using the public lavatory. I cannot live in a government bungalow, that is why some of us are still living in Bukom. So those of us who live in Bukom should try and make our homes our bungalows. Progress, that is what it is. That is what Kwame said. So who are you to come and tell me I cannot build a good toilet in my own house?'

'But Kwame Nkrumah himself made the law,' explained Mr Lamptey.

'Kwame Nkrumah is not an ass. He will not bring a foolish law like that to Bukom. If there is such a law, it is meant for lizards like you who close your eyes and point your left hands towards where your roots are. I am going to build this thing and if you misbehave, I am going to see that you lose your jobs. It is people like you who try to sabotage the good work of the Osagyefo.' Ataa Kojo was now speaking with a tone of authority.

The man could not help noticing it. He heard what Ataa Kojo had threatened. He had no way of knowing whether Ataa Kojo was one of the party's fanatics who, though they did not sit in parliament, wielded such authority as to effect the dismissal of an official under any pretext. He himself had seen it done and if he had a good head on his shoulders he would be careful how he dealt with this man.

'I'm sorry, but it seems you've got me all wrong. I did not say you could not carry on the work. All I'm saying is that you should get papers for it.'

'What papers?'

'The city council can give you those papers if you apply.'

'Is that so?'

'Yes.'

'I see. Now these papers, why don't you get them for me? After all, your clan and mine are closely related. The Lampteys have always been known to be good people; that's why they always had good education.' Suddenly he asked. 'Are you related to the lawyer?'

'He is my uncle. His brother, the doctor, is my father.'

'Ah, now see, we are related. I know your father. Look, we all played together as kids; it's only that they had more brains and their father had horses.'

'Yes.'

'Well, you get me those papers, like a good lad,' Ataa Kojo instructed.

Mr Lamptey said he would and promised to send people to come and survey the layout for the necessary plan to be drawn and submitted. He dug his hands into his pocket, sought out a note and gave it to Ataa Kojo.

'Here, you may buy tobacco with this.'

'Oh, thank you, thank you. You are really a son of a Lamptey,' Ataa Kojo thanked him.

Plan and permit for the structure were presented to Ataa Kojo in three days and he had no more trouble from the city council.

Progress on the construction was not steady as Ataa Kojo relied, financially, entirely on monthly contributions from his children. Chico was the one who bore the brunt of inconvenience caused by the project. And as long as Martey sent money through the old man, he would not get his pocket money. He therefore wrote to his brother in Takoradi.

Dear brother Martey,

I am sure this letter will come as a pleasant surprise since I have not written to you for such a long time. Well, as you may imagine, the responsibility the school placed on my head is so enormous that I hardly find time to write letters. But as William Shakespeare said, "Uneasy lies the head that wears the crown" I am sure you know that quotation.

Bill Marshall

Well, I visited the house last week and found work going on well on Ataa Kojo's flush toilet. He is so involved with the project that he would even scrape his head bald and sell his hair if he could find someone to buy it. For this reason, he refused to give me the money you sent him for my pocket and other personal requirements. It is almost impossible to make him see that education is more important than a flush toilet. But, sometimes, I do not want to blame him. He seems to be dedicated to this project. It looks as if his life depends on it. Perhaps he knows what he is doing. But what he is doing is not good for me.

For instance, last month, it was Maami Adoley who gave me money to buy a pair of trunks and boots for sports. That woman has been very very kind to me. She is now almost like a mother to me. Only last week, she sent me gari, sugar, and milk. I hope that one day, I will be able to repay her kindness. For the meantime, however, I do not wish to depend on her too much. I shall therefore be grateful if you kindly send my remittance directly to me and not through Ataa Kojo for I will never get it as long as his project is unfinished. So please brother, send it to me directly through the college or care of P.O.Box 1203, Accra. That box belongs to the father of one of my friends and I always write letters through it.

And lastly, how are you? I hope you are fine and will send me the money direct. You will be glad to know that I have won the inter-college table tennis championship for

Zone 3. I am training hard to win the whole Accra College Championship trophy at the end of the academic year.

Well, brother, there is nothing more to say but to end this letter, hoping that you will send the money soon to relieve me of my predicament.

Give my regards to all
Your little brother
Chico.

Chapter 12

The universal processes of man's existence have always been constant, for even in the face of modern technology, man still opens the earth and plants his seeds. The rains come down and the seeds germinate. Man smiles and prays for more so that the plant may grow, and the flowers bear fruits so that he may pluck it and feed on its juice or matter.

Fofo did not smile when she realised that a seed had taken root in her womb. She would perhaps have smiled if she had planted the seed there herself. It was true that she had offered her womanhood to a man, but the actual planting had not been done by her.

It was almost six weeks since she last saw any blood and although she had taken her normal periods for granted, she now had cause to miss the flow. She had not thought of pregnancy when she paid subsequent visits to Larry's place. The magnet whose force pulled her there was that natural female urge to get more from the source where the first one came from. Larry had opened her up for the first time and since she knew no other, it was simple sense always to visit the scene of the crime.

She was particularly quiet that day. She had got up that morning with an unexpected nausea. Her father heard her vomiting in the compound.

'What's the matter with you, Fofo?'

'Nothing.'

'Nothing?'

'Yes.'

'Then stop vomiting,' he said.

Fofo had a bad day at the office that day and when she closed, she did not go home. Instead, she went to Larry's place. She sat quietly and talked little.

'You're quiet today, Fofo,' he remarked.

'I'm not well.'

'What's the matter with you?'

'I missed my period last month,' she said.

'What?'

'I said I missed my period.'

'Oh,' Larry said, not knowing exactly what he meant himself or what he meant Fofo to take the 'Oh' for.

There was silence for some moments, during which you could hear the boy's heartbeat if you listened hard enough.

'So you'd better do what you want to do,' Fofo said, breaking the silence.

'What do you mean?'

'Well, you are responsible for it.'

'I have not denied it, have I?

'Then do what you want to do because very soon people will begin to notice it.'

'What do you want me to do?'

'Well, it's up to you. As for me, I don't want people to talk about me and at Bukom, people talk.'

'Now what are you saying, Fofo, for God's sake?' Larry asked, almost shouting.

'Dammit, man, don't shout at me like that. What do you think I am? You slept with me and made me pregnant. Now you want to shout at me on top of it?' Fofo was angry.

'There is no need to be angry, I was not shouting. I only want your suggestions, that's all.'

'What suggestion?' she asked.'

'Well, what you think is the best way out. After all, this thing is only six weeks old.'

'Two months, man, two months!!'

'But you said… well, so it is two months.'

'And I'm not going for an abortion so think of what you're going to do.'

'Hmm…the thing is that I can't marry you, not now.'

'But you slept with me, didn't you? Do you know exactly what happens to a woman if you nap with her?'

'I think you know how to protect yourself.'

'Don't talk nonsense. How to protect myself indeed! What do you take me for – a prostitute, I suppose.'

The boy was rather shaken by Fofo's outburst. Maybe he had used the wrong words. There is always a way around this sort of situation if only the right words could be found.

'Well, Fofo, the truth is that I'm planning to go abroad for further studies and this thing has come at the wrong time. I would like to marry you but not at the moment. It will spoil everything I have planned for the past years.'

'So I should get rid of it?'

'I have not said that.'

'Then what are you saying?'

'Fofo, try to understand.'

'The only thing I understand now is that I am pregnant and you are responsible for it.'

'Yes, yes, but for God's sake, give me time to think!'

'Time to think?'

'Yes, hell.'

'All right, Take as long as you like to think. When you've finished thinking, you can come to my home and tell me.' Fofo said and left the room.

Lawrence buried his head in his hands. He was the man. He had penetrated the ground and sowed the seed. The seed had been watered and it had germinated. If he were a farmer, he would pray for more rains. But he was not a farmer, and he had not put any seed in the ground. He had slept with a woman and the woman was now pregnant. He had not planned the pregnancy. He had not even planned the initial sexual intercourse. It had come, as it were naturally to both of them on the night of the boat race. And now, he was more of a victim than the woman who was going to carry the baby in her womb for nine months or thereabouts.

But if she had an operation now, she would not have to carry any baby, and he Lawrence, would carry a heavy conscience the rest of his life. He could try to forget about it when he went to England. But he was not made of that kind of tough fabric. He was a guy all right, but he was also a Christian. He valued human life, both his and that of others.

All right, Fofo could have the baby. The baby should bear his name, but all that would not stop him from going to England. All he would have to do is to mind how he spent his money and to make the relevant adjustments in his plans.

He gave himself twenty-four hours to reformulate those plans. Then he would go and see Fofo and tell her to take it easy, for all would be well, for he still loved her and that was all that mattered for other things would sort themselves out. He would have liked to get up, jump on his scooter drive to Fofo's home, but tempers were not very good that night. He would wait till the following day, give her time to cool down a bit. Women were usually reasonably receptive when their tempers were good. So he would let some cool air blow over the blow-up. Lets wait till tomorrow.

Tomorrow did come. At the end of the day, Larry drove straight home from work. He had a bath and rested for a while. Then, when it was dark, he put on a clean shirt and drove to Bukom. It was almost seven o'clock when he arrived there but Fofo had not returned home.

He parked his scooter and decided to wait. He took up a position some yards away from the house and from which he could see the entrance to the house.

About half an hour later, a taxi pulled to a stop in front of the house. Out of it stepped Fofo.

'Pssst!' Larry tried to attract her attention, but Fofo ignored it, thinking that it was only the usual catcalls for which the Bukom boys are notorious.

'Fofo!' he called.

She stopped.

Larry emerged from the dark and walked towards her. She recognised him. 'Oh, it's you.'

'I've been waiting for the past hour,' he began, exaggerating the duration of his waiting a little.

'Have you finished thinking?'

'Listen, Fofo, I have decided that you should let the thing stay because I have decided to marry you.'

'What did you say?' Fofo asked, pretending not to have heard.

'Aw, come on, Fofo, don't make things difficult for me. I said you should let the thing stay.'

'Well, it's too late, I've got rid of it,' she said. 'I had an abortion,' she added.

Anger rushed into the boy's eyes and before Fofo could guess his intentions, he slapped her, jolting her head sideways. She screamed and tried to run away from the assault, but the boy grabbed her arm and twisted it behind her back in a wrestling grip. Fofo screamed for help, and presently people gathered round them, asking what the matter was.

'Ask her!' the boy said.

'Ha, she took your money and would not give you her tokuro, eh?' somebody cracked. There was laughter from the small crowd. The noise in the street attracted Ataa Kojo from the house. He pushed his way through the crowd.

'Fofo, what is the matter? He asked.

'He was beating me,' she replied pointing at the angry boy.

'Hey, young man, what's the matter?'

'He was beating me,' she repeated.

'All right, come home,' he said, then turning to the boy, he added, 'You'd better come too.'

The boy followed them, reluctantly, into the house.

He sat.

'Now what is the matter and why were you beating up my daughter in the street like that?'

'She can tell you better. Ask her.'

The old man turned to his daughter. 'Did you take his money?' he asked.

'No.'

'Then why was he beating you?'

Fofo did not reply.

'Well, you see, Fofo and I have been friends for some months now,' Larry began.

'Tsu!' Fofo interrupted.

'Shut up, Fofo!'

'Well, as I said, we have been friends and she …well… last night she came to my house and told me that…well…'

'Told you what?'

'Err…well, she told me that she was pregnant,' the boy managed to say.

'I see. Is that why you were beating her?'

'No. She has had an abortion.'

'That's a lie!' Fofo denied.

'Fofo!'

'That's a lie, father, it's not true.'

'Then why is he saying that when it is not true?'

'I've not had any abortion.'

'So you are pregnant?'

'I'm not pregnant.'

'Dammit, you told me you were.' The boy confronted her.

'But you said you did not want it.'

'I did not say that.'

'Then what did you say?' Ataa Kojo asked.

'Think, think! When you were sleeping with me, were you not thinking?'

'Shut up, Fofo!' Ataa Kojo ordered. Then turning to the boy, he asked again why he was beating her.

'Well, I came to tell her that I would marry her so she should not worry about the pregnancy. She then told me that she had already had an abortion.'

'I have not had an abortion!'

'Then why did you tell him you had?'

'Just to make him angry.'

'So you are pregnant?' Ataa Kojo asked.

Fofo was silent.

'I knew you were pregnant. You thought I was born yesterday? Well, I was not born yesterday, you know, I heard you vomiting a couple of days ago. When I asked you, you said there was nothing wrong with you.' Then, turning to the boy, he said, ' So what are you going to do?'

The boy admitted responsibility but explained his plans to go abroad.

'I hope when I've gone, I will be able to let Fofo join me. She can study to be a seamstress or a secretary.'

'Well, then you'd better ask your people to come and perform the necessary customary rites for engagement. And it had better be soon, otherwise I will take a serious view of the fact that you have made my daughter pregnant without my knowledge. You know, by tradition, that amounts to theft.'

'I know, sir, but it was a slip.'

'Nonsense, sleeping with a woman is not a slip, it is an act.'

'Yes, sir.' He said and got up.

'I beg to leave, sir.'

'All right, good night.'

'Good night sir.' He made for the entrance. Fofo got up and followed him.

'Why did you tell me you had an abortion?' he asked when they were outside the house.

Fofo informed him that, as a matter of fact, she had planned to get rid of it and that was why she was late in coming home. A friend at her office had taken her to a doctor after work and she had been given an appointment for the following day. The friend had told her that this 'doctor' was good and had been doing it for girls even when the thing was four months old.

'As for you, you are so stupid you would believe anything.' Larry said.

'Yes, so stupid I would believe you would take me to the U.K. even…'

'Fofo, when I said that I was not just talking, I have planned the whole thing. Listen, let's go to my place and I will explain it all.'

'But it is late.'

'Doesn't matter, I will bring you back.'

'Where is the scooter?'

'Over there,' he said.

Fofo spent that night at Larry's place.

Chapter 13

Do not cry, my baby, do not cry
And let someone see your mouth.
For your teeth are gold
And your tongue silk
Do not cry, my baby, do not cry.
Do not cry, my baby, do not cry
And let someone see your mouth
Are you hungry
Or your stomach is aching?
Do not cry, my baby, do not cry

Fofo sang the lullaby over and over again, enjoying it so much herself that she did not even realise that the baby in her arms had stopped crying and was fast asleep.

'The child is asleep, Fofo, why don't you put him to bed?' Karley said.

She had come from Kumasi to take care of her younger sister and the baby. She was excited about the baby. Maami Adoley had offered her services and had come to the house every morning to bath the child and powder her. She had insisted Fofo had enough rest as she prepared her light soup dosed with red pepper. She said it was good for mothers for it helped cure the sore in the stomach. But now she had stopped coming to the house because, for one thing, her own health had not been in the best of states; and for another, since the arrival of Fofo's own sister from Kumasi, she could reduce the frequency of her visits and see after her own health. She had had a surgical operation performed on her some years earlier to remove a cyst from her stomach. Now it seemed that she needed another operation. There had been gossip that she was a witch and that when they opened her stomach, they had found a tortoise in it. But Ataa Kojo knew it was all foolish gossip and that it was absolutely safe for her to come and help look after Fofo and the child.

'Is the baby comfortable?' Karley asked when Fofo returned from the room.

'Yes.'

'Well, then you'd better go and sit on the hot water.'

'Oh, God, how I dread sitting on this hot water.'

'Well, you'd better get used to it because every mother has to take her medication seriously. If you don't sit on the hot water regularly, your wound will not heal,' she cautioned.

'Tsu!' Fofo said and fetched the boiling water from the fire.

The baby was six weeks old and the father had performed the outdooring ceremony before leaving for England. He planned everything carefully and Fofo's confidence in him was absolute. He had written two letters from London and had informed Fofo that all was going well. His uncle at the Ghana High Commission was arranging for a government scholarship for him and very soon he would be a full-time student and leave his job at the railways. A parcel was on the way and she was to get in touch with Mr Okai of Ghana Airways for it. When the time came, this Mr Okai would help her obtain her passport and visa.

He missed her and the baby so much and hoped she was taking good care of herself. Any time the baby was ill, she was to inform his elder brother at T.V.C. office.

She was to send Chico's neck size for he would like to send him a shirt for Christmas.

The last message thrilled Chico to bits.

'Did he not ask for the size of shoes I wear?'

'No! And I don't want you writing begging letters to him,' Fofo warned.

'Oh, I was going to ask him to find a school for me in England. I want to go and do engineering,' Chico said.

'You can do that at the Technology in Kumasi.'

'You are selfish.'

'Nonsense!'

Chico had been made the senior prefect at the school, following a college scandal involving the former head prefect. The onus of the end of year speech therefore fell on Chico's shoulders. But he knew he could make a good job of it. He was chairman of the college debating society and his speeches had often elicited applause and cheers. He knew that he could get an ovation on the Speech Day.

He had only to prepare for the day. And he had the peace of mind to do it, for he had no more problems over pocket money. The monthly remittances from his brother had come to him direct – thanks to his well-worded letter. If only he had written much earlier. But not to worry, he now had enough in his pocket. All he needed was a kente cloth.

'I will get you a kente cloth if it is the last thing I can do,' Ataa Kojo promised.

But Chico knew that he could not take his father's word for it. The toilet was still under construction, and although it was near completion, he could not see his father conjuring money from anywhere to buy a kente cloth. He therefore went to Maami Adoley.

'Don't you worry your head over it. If kente is all you want, then rest your heart. I can give you one. I want you to appear nice on that day. I shall be there myself to clap for you. Then you will know that I'm really proud of you, Chico,' the woman said.

'Thank you, Maami Adoley.'

The weeks passed and the time for the speech day drew nearer. As she had promised, Maami Adoley gave Chico a kente cloth. She said she would be there. Her health was not getting any better and she had even stopped selling kenkey. But she would be there if she had to crawl.

'I want you to be there. I would like you to come early so that you can sit in the front row for me to see you. Maami Adoley, I will be able to speak better if I see you in the front row,' he said.

'I will be there.'

On the morning of the Speech Day, Ataa Kojo got up very early. He said he was going to see his friend at the Ga Mantse palace. He did not come back till the afternoon. He was holding a parcel. He was stone drunk. And when Fofo told him that people for the Water Works had come to connect the water into the toilet, he showed no sign of pleasure.

'What's the matter, Ataa Kojo?'

'Is everything all right with you children?' he asked.

'Yes, they have connected water into the toilet,' Fofo repeated.

'Yes, you said that before,' he said and staggered into his room.

'That is strange,' Fofo remarked.

'Yes indeed. I thought he would jump into the sky.'

'But what's the matter with him?'

'He is drunk.'

'Yes, but there is something more on his mind. He looked sad.'

When the old man returned from the room, he was dressed in his white suit, complete with his gold tie-pin.

'Where are you going to?' Karley asked.

'Chico's Speech Day is to-day,' he said.

'And this parcel?'

'It is a kente cloth. He said he wanted a kente cloth.'

'Where did you buy it?'

'I did not buy it. I borrowed it from a friend at the Ga Mantse's palace.'

'Is anything the matter, Ataa Kojo?'

'It is Maami Adoley across the road. She is dead. But I must go and give this kente cloth to Chico at school. I'm almost late.' He left the house, the parcel under his arm.

***

Allotey must have had the blessing of the gods that day. He had that morning narrowly missed being thrown in a police cell for owing his landlord months of rent arrears. Life outside the family house had not been as he had expected. Living on one's own, he now realised, demanded more than just a wish to be independent.

When he left the family house at Bukom, he had taken a room in Adabraka. He had spent all his little savings on a bedstead, a few chairs and a centre table. And having to pay the rent every month, foot the electricity bill, and eat out, made it impossible to continue paying installments on the wireless set he had bought on hire-purchase.

A threatening letter from the radio dealer had forced him to borrow money to make up the payment. He had subsequently used his rent money to pay off the loan. A situation in which the landlord had no hand. All he wanted was his rent. And when he had not been getting it for three months, he resorted to the only method he knew to be effective in the circumstances.

Allotey was in the room when he heard a knock on the door. He suspected that the caller was his landlord. He was right. It was his landlord, and with him was a police constable.

'Here he is,' the landlord told the constable, by pointing at Allotey.

'Oh, so you are Mr Allotey?'

'Yes.'

'Well, you'd better come to station with me,' the constable said.

'Oh, please, but I will pay.'

'Don't mind him, officer, he is always telling me I will pay, I will pay, but he does not pay. For the past three month, he has been telling me this story over and over.'

'All right, Mr Allotey, are coming with me, or do you want me to use force?' the constable asked.

Allotey looked at the size of the constable and decided that if the man used force, he (Allotey) would get the worse of it.

'All right.' He got up and followed them to the police station.

The charge office was a dark little office, and the cell just behind the counter was much darker. From where he stood, he could see two people pacing the floor in the cell. He could not see their faces but their eyes shone like those of a tiger in a cage.

'Sergeant, we have come, sir,' the police officer reported to the charge officer who was in an adjacent office.

'All right, I'm coming,' he said when he finally emerged, he turned out to be Sergeant Papoe, whom Allotey knew in the Bukom neighbourhood.

'Oh, Allotey, is that you?' he asked.

'Yes,' Allotey replied quickly.

'Oh, too bad,' he lamented.

'You know him?' the constable asked the sergeant.

'Yes, we both come from Bukom in James Town.'

'Well, I think this is home palava.' Then turning to the landlord, he told him that it would be best if the matter was settled in his office.

'No, I want this man put inside to teach him a lesson,' the landlord said.

'Look here, who told you that you can put a man in a cell for owing you just three months rent?' the sergeant shouted.

'But that is what you told me.'

'Look, my friend, I told you nothing, if you don't take care, I will put you in the cell for false accusation.

'What?'

'Yes.'

'And my money?'

'What money?'

'I gave some money to…'

'To whom? Look, take care, my friend otherwise you'll see something, you hear?'

'My God!'

'Look, don't you come calling God's name like this in here. You think this place is church?'

Eventually, the landlord left the station, swearing to throw Allotey's things out of the room.'

'Listen, you cannot do this. That will be causing damage to property!'

'We shall see!'

When the landlord left, the sergeant asked Allotey why he went and hired a room when there was his family house.

'You boys don't like peace of mind. You are always going out to find trouble. I will advise you to go and pack and go back to Bukom. After all, your landlord has a case, you know? And if you had been somebody else, I would have had you thrown inside.'

And so Allotey hurried to his room, packed all his things in a suitcase and took a taxi to Bukom.

For the second time that day, luck was on his side because Ataa Kojo was not there to ask questions. If he returned in the evening to find him there, he could not throw him out of the house. After all, it was he who said one could not leave one's roots.

***

Ataa Kojo arrived at the school's assembly hall when Chico was getting to the end of his speech. The old man stood in the doorway of the main entrance and the evening sun cast a long shadow of his figure on the floor.

Chico recognised him and paused in his speech. This drew the attention of the entire assembly to the solitary figure standing in the doorway.

Then Chico continued:

'Fellow students, ladies and gentlemen, with determination and sacrifice, it is possible to achieve anything, almost anything in this world. My old man taught me that. As I leave this college, I do so with the pride that I have been a product of the finest school in this country. I also do so with the hope that the honour placed on me by the authorities of this school has been worthwhile. That is to say I hope I have discharged my duty creditably. And if I leave, then permit me to express my sincere gratitude to all the masters of this institution whose advice and guidance have helped me to carry out the tasks of a head prefect. I will also like to thank my fellow students through whose co-operation my duty has been possible. And if through this duty, I have incurred the anger or malice of anybody, this is the time for me to say, please forgive me and forget for it was all in the interest of this great college of Onus.

Now, before I sit down, ladies and gentlemen, let me introduce to you my father.'

There was great applause as Chico pointed out the solitary figure in the doorway. And as the applause continued, Ataa Kojo wondered whether it was for him or his son. He smiled and walked towards the rostrum.

Chico stepped down and walked towards his father. When they met, Ataa Kojo embraced his son.

'That's my boy,' he said, his voice shaking.

'What's the matter?'

'You make me proud, Chico,' he said.

'Where is Maami Adoley?' Chico asked.

'Let's go outside, Chico,' Ataa Kojo said, put his hand on Chico's shoulder, and led him outside.

'Maami Adoley said she would come.'

'Chico, she cannot come. Chico, Maami Adoley died this morning,' his father said.

Chico stood still. His eyes began to fill with tears. The kente cloth Maami Adoley had given him for the Speech Day dropped and fell from his shoulders. Ataa Kojo noticed it for the first time.

'I brought you the kente,' he said.

'I had one. Maami Adoley gave me this one. Maybe she came after all. Maybe she clapped for me,' Chico said with a hard smile, and allowed the tears to roll down his cheeks.

Printed in the United States
By Bookmasters